CALL INTO NOWHERE

Vladislav Temkin

In memories of my mother

Table of Contents

PART 1

Instead of a Prologue:
"Santa Maria," "Pinta," and "Niña"

"People carried within them a soul-chilling, seemingly unreachable yet warmly persistent hope, a hope to conquer themselves, overcome harsh reality, become better, and touch unknown happiness... That hope was taken from them by the revolution. And happiness? Happiness was replaced by hysterical merriment, orchestrated by efficient, pragmatic killers. That's the essence of the novel *Running on Waves*, summarized Sveridov, dropping his half-empty beer mug onto the table with a thud.

I tried to keep up: "But what about romanticism?" I asked, ordering another pint.

"Romanticism? Where do you see romanticism in this swamp?" he retorted. "Or are you going to point me toward other books or fantasies?" Sveridov wasn't letting it go.

He'd obviously had too much to drink. It had been a rough day; our tourist bus lost a wheel at full speed and nearly tumbled into Lake Geneva. At first, something rattled like a winch...

The wind howled violently. But the driver ignored passengers' complaints. The wheel broke loose and rolled across to the opposite side of the road, narrowly missing cars speeding past. The bus scraped to a halt on its right flank, sending up a shower of sparks from the sturdy Swiss asphalt.

"We're on fire!" someone shouted, as people began pounding their fists against the windows and doors...

Eventually, the bus came to a stop. We stumbled out onto the sidewalk, shaken by fear, yet strangely elated by our narrow escape.

Sveridov had once been my professor at the Medical Institute. By sheer coincidence, I ran into him on that ill-fated trip through Austria and Switzerland. Drunk and disheveled, I helped him back to his hotel room, where, on parting, he tossed me a reflection:

"You know, Volodya, all people fall into two categories. Some are certain that two times two equals five... Others know it's four—but that knowledge annoys them. You're a good guy, Volodya, but there's threading in your head." He paused, then added with a knowing look, "And you're aware of it."

"Well, at least I remember the names of Columbus's three ships from his first voyage to *Terra Incognita!*" I shouted at the door as it slammed shut in front of my face.

Then, with no hope left, I whispered quietly:

"Santa Maria, Pinta, and Niña."

On the Threshold

Gunshots cracked through the air, sending cawing crows skyward. Two strangers kept firing, again and again. Several black bodies dropped onto the cobblestones below. I leaned out the window, curious to see who had shattered the silence.

Out on the street, the two men were reloading their pistols, mocking each other with smug grins. They showed no intention of ending the slaughter.

Balconies filled with onlookers, idle and stunned. Some shouted in outrage, "How could anyone shoot at such helpless birds?" But the two weren't moved by these defenders of nature. Even threats to call the police left them unfazed.

They only began to settle down when everything had been scrambled by someone's rough, merciless hand. My second postdoctoral journey was an exact replica of the first, and that, in turn, hardly differed from the grueling pursuit of a third degree.

Or was there truly a difference? A question irrelevant to the corrupt, hypocritical judges who assigned spies to monitor me

I'm not boasting about my degrees. It's just that, apart from them and the unrelenting lack of freedom that stalks me, I have nothing at forty-five. No wife, no children, no friends, no home, no job.

Only my mother remains. And the guilt I carry toward her poisons my existence no less than living in a shell.

Weakness doesn't always deserve pity, especially when it refuses to accept even well-meant criticism. Though even our enemies, at times, deserve credit for the sharp but accurate words they throw our way.

I fell just short of victory. In the final moments, I was utterly defeated, even though the Sisyphean task was nearly complete. The article glimmered on the horizon, like Ithaca before Odysseus, so close, yet still out of reach. And then, someone either through carelessness or malicious intent unleashed a merciless wind. Now, there's nowhere to seek mercy or leniency. My fate, and the fate of the article, is sealed. The manuscript is bound either for the trash bin... or to feed the egos of the powerful.

As for me? It seems I'm destined to entertain the public for the rest of my days...

"Do I feel broken and betrayed once again in this life?"
A question posed by the so-called *psycho-anatomists*, tactlessly poking through my existence like surgeons probing a raw wound.

I write these lines in the evenings, thinking that tomorrow will bring a new day. But alas, it never offers me anything joyful. That's how I lived for five years in San Francisco.

"Tomorrow will be different," I used to lull myself with that thought during my brief and lonely moments of rest.

But each *tomorrow* brought fresh battles over my projects, petty complications, the constant dread of looming deadlines, and experiment after experiment after experiment...

For the first two years, I didn't see the sea, or rather, the ocean, even once. I slept on the floor, on an inflatable mattress. My room didn't even have furniture, only unopened boxes scattered in the dark, which I kept bumping into, looming here and there

Yes, it truly was a life in confinement. But at the time, I had no idea what real captivity meant. It's not so terrifying to live under guard when you know that beyond the high fences, life, pure and unrestrained, like a mountain stream, still flows, despite the bumps and cracks in the path. What's far worse is when you can no longer tell where the prison ends and freedom begins, when you lose not just your independence and hope, but your very sanity.

Better to bow to what is
to the given,
with its fleeting, narrow paths,

which one day
will seem to you,
strangely, so vast,
They will seem vast—
dusty, strewn with compromise—
they will seem like mighty wings,
they will seem like great birds.
Yes. It's better to bow to what is,
with its meager measurements,
which, in the end
to the extreme
will serve you as railings
(not especially clean ones),
holding in balance
your limping truths
on this chipped staircase

—*Joseph Brodsky*

I entered the "dead zone", that's what we called the narrow corridor connecting Professor Sergio Kainman's office with the office of his lab director (Jacqueline), the secretary's office, and the computer room.

Quietly closing the door behind him, the blond Hans emerged from Kainman's office wearing the smile of a python that had just swallowed a rabbit... I wondered, what could possibly make someone smile like that after meeting with a boss who, in five years, hadn't produced a single chart, a single image, hadn't achieved any results in his so-called project?.. As if reading my mind, Hans threw at me:-

"In Kainman's laboratory, survival is a personal struggle, each person finds their own way to endure."

"In Kainman's lab, everyone survives however they can..."

"And how do you survive?" I asked, reluctantly drawn into a pointless, meaningless conversation.

"Very soon, Volodya, you'll find out..." Hans laughed and vanished down the corridor, his lab coat rustling behind him.

"What an idiot," I muttered, unsure of whom I was more irritated, him or myself!?

I sat down at the computer, scanned a photograph, and stared blankly at the electrophoresis image that appeared on the Photoshop screen...

"If only I could jump a couple of years into the future..." I thought.

"Granted!" shouted a little man from the computer, dressed in a black frock coat and a matching silk bow tie.

I rubbed my eyes, but the little man didn't vanish. He just winked at me cheerfully.

He was reading my thoughts.

Thus continued our strange, almost absurd conversation, I'd think, and he'd say it out loud. Back then, I had no idea that such dialogues would become the norm in my not-so-cheerful life. Or maybe they had already happened before... ten, maybe fifteen years ago?

"2012? Okay, no problem..."

"You're reading my thoughts, and now you want to send me to the future? That's nonsense... And what about my photograph? Where did it go?"

"Your photo isn't going anywhere. But moving into the future... I can actually make that happen. Here's the deal, I'll start counting down from ten."

"Wait! What about my experiments?"

"Nine, eight... soon you won't need them anymore..."

"But I'm still wearing my lab coat..."

"Five, four... Where you're going, they'll give you a new one, crisp and white. And not just the coat," the little man in black chuckled.

"But I haven't warned anyone here that I'm leaving, that I'm traveling to another time."

"Soon, 'another time' will become your true and only reality. Whether you'll like it or not, that's up to you... or maybe not just you," he added thoughtfully.

"Two, one... And may all the rising and falling stars, bright and dim, shine for you," the strange little man in the computer said at last. "Feel their distant warmth, if you can understand what I mean..."

When the starless feeling of drifting away
from those shores where dawns were once met with hope,
my dear friend,
by God, there's no need to despair—
believe in the unknown,
frighteningly black pier.

Not scary up close

A frighteningly dark pier.
Up close, it's not so scary
what often frightens us from afar.
There too are eyes, voices,
and flickers of cigarette lights.
You grow a little accustomed,
and the creak of that ghostly dock
will tell you
there is no such thing as the only harbor.

—Yevgeny Yevtushenko

The Beginning

The alarm clock rang. From the kitchen came my mother's commanding voice:

"Volodya, are you going to work or not?"

"Where am I? What work?" I got up reluctantly from the bed. Washed my face, got dressed.

My mother handed me my backpack.

"I packed your breakfast. Don't forget to drink water." She moved over to the phone. It was Nina, my mother's friend, calling.

Nina had married an ultra-Orthodox religious man, and now she and my mother shared only two topics of conversation: the war and the harsh childhood that followed. Occasionally, they'd slip in a few Yiddish words—but always made sure to explain them to each other.

I stepped outside.

"So now what? Where do I go?"

A high-speed tram shot past with a long, piercing screech like a bird's cry. Suddenly, a passerby turned to face me and said,

"You need the thirty-ninth bus. That way." He waved his hand toward the nearest stop.

It's worth noting that on the way to the hospital with the resonant name "Soroka," several strangers called out to me on the street and on public transport, directing me where to go...

Somehow, I made it to the Faculty of Pharmacology. At the door stood Professor Filippovich, whom I knew from my third-degree studies. He greeted me cheerfully, shook my hand firmly, and gave me a thumbs-up—as if to say everything was fine. He also said that I...

I was told to go up to the sixth floor, to the laboratory of Dr. William Roshti (not yet a professor). Dr. Roshti greeted me with a sour smile. He invited me to sit down and offered coffee. I took a seat on a chair next to the table, but politely declined the coffee.

"Life as a postdoc isn't easy," Roshti lectured. "But if you don't succeed, it gets downright cruel."

"I have a paper under review," I foolishly replied.

"Why do you need that?" Roshti continued. "Even if you get published, then you have to secure a grant and that's no simple task..."

"I can submit a scientific proposal..."

"Sure, you can submit it, but who's going to give you the money?" William laughed, baring his crooked teeth, then immediately fell silent, lost in his own thoughts.

"So, what do you suggest?" I asked.

"You can continue working on your project in my lab... But I'm only here temporarily until the funding runs out. Then you will be on your own..."

"I've heard this somewhere before..." I said aloud.

"But who's going to finish the paper?"

"Someone will finish it, no doubt..."

"Well, that 'someone' will be the first author on the paper."

"Which matters more to you, the work or the paper? If you don't make it in this lab, you won't make it anywhere..."

"I've heard that somewhere before... This paper is mine, just as much as Sergio Kainman's, my supervisor during my second postdoc. I worked with him for five years. He earned the right to be the corresponding and last author."

"I'm not going to talk to Sergio," I said stubbornly, looking Roshti in the eye.

"That's not required from you," he said with irritation, looking away. "Fine, get to work. And make sure you don't pick fights with anyone..."

> *The dark bonds of earthly captivity*
> *I could not overcome by any means,*
> *And with a heavy shell of scorn*
> *I am shackled from head to toe.*

—Osip Mandelstam

I entered a narrow, small room where wooden tables with metal legs, covered in white, glossy paper, almost touched each other. I had been here before... but I couldn't recall when exactly. Probably before leaving Concordia for America. Yes, that's right, I worked here while studying for my second and third degrees.

I remembered Amy, how she used to tease me about my Russian-Concordia accent. We met at the university. I had come into the room next to her laboratory by mistake and walked into her office while she was working at the computer. We started talking, and I began visiting her often. Neither of us had anyone in Denver, which brought us closer. One day, Amy invited me to a Christmas party. I gladly accepted. At the party, we danced a lot. During a slow dance, she pressed close to me, and I found myself wanting to do with her what we ended up doing for the next two years.

In those two years, Amy didn't change, but I changed her. The shy but principled girl who didn't know how to kiss was gone without a trace. Amy began looking around, sizing up men and women, gossiping. Calculations crept into her actions...

That summer, we went to Yellowstone National Park. I never let go of the steering wheel. For several days, a fierce, pouring rain battered us. The wipers struggled to sweep away the slanting rain mercilessly lashing the windows of our small jeep. We drove seven to eight hours a day. Sitting behind the wheel in those conditions was exhausting.

Later, a Chinese guy named Peter, from William Roshti's lab, tested me: "Apparently, his 'friend'... was on vacation in Yellowstone. For some reason, this 'friend' wouldn't let his girlfriend drive the car."

I blurted out, "Well, maybe his 'friend' is a real gentleman..."

I hold no grudge against Amy for those details. I understand what "methods" were used to gather "evidence" against me...

Two years later, Amy's boss got a lucrative offer, and Amy moved with him to Boston. We often called each other, but spent long moments in silence on the phone. She was silent from pain; I from politeness.

"In the fall, I'll come to Denver," Amy once told me.

"For long?"

"I don't know…"

But fall came, and Amy called less and less. She never came to Denver. Once, she called and said she was going through "big changes," but she would tell me about them later…

Two weeks before her wedding, Amy finally gathered the courage to tell me she was getting married. I congratulated her.

The bus pulls away from the station. Someone…

The bus pulls away from the station,
Someone waves as if beckoning a friend.
Someday, I might feel unwell,
But surely, it won't be because of you.

And now, the road stretches far ahead…
The sleepy sun bids me farewell.
A pink trail falls from the sky
No, I will never see you again.

Deserted fields and a gloomy town
Lie between us, unaware of harm.
A stranger's bed looms at the doorstep
Yet I will remember you for a long time.

My thoughts were interrupted by Dr. Roshti's cheeky student, Dusty:

"Listen! Your ex-girlfriend's husband is still waiting for you."

Hmm... She reads my thoughts too. Let's test that again. I thought to myself, "Yesterday, I read on the BBC website that the London Olympics are being protected by girls..."

"That's rude to think..." Dusty snapped. "And anyway, if you don't focus on Sergio Kainman, you won't get any results in your experiments."

Outside the window, a pigeon was preening its white-gray feathers, wings spread wide.

Someone startled it, and it flew away. Maybe if I don't spill all of Kainman's secrets, they'll kick me out.

But if I do spill them, they'll kick me out even faster

made man, yet your fate remains enticing:
a lifetime spent on a journey,
and only one thing pulls you from sleep—
where do we go
when spring rages behind our backs?

—Bulat Okudzhava

So, the news on the radio, TV, and internet is fabricated... or altered... From the corridor emerged Professor Yossi Zlokherson, clad in a black cloak that draped from his narrow shoulders almost to the floor. Zlokherson was taller than average, about six feet one inch. Though his glasses lent him an air of intellect, those who knew him well understood that familiarity was unwelcome.

Zlokherson's inquisitive brown eyes bored into you with such piercing intensity that his interlocutor would feel... uneasy. Zlokherson nodded at me, almost peaceably—as peaceful as he could be—and then walked away.

Dusty didn't let up:

"If you keep going like this, you won't get rid of uninvited guests in your apartment."

"I'm the uninvited guest myself only in my own country," I finally muttered.

"That can be fixed quickly. Want to get into Zelotania? Look out the window."

On the neighboring hill, a minaret rose in the middle of the village like a lonely chisel stuck in an empty, toothless mouth.

"How's the view? They'll quickly show you what's what there..."

"I don't want to go to Zelotania," I said.

"Then control your thoughts.

And don't you dare think I'll of the French."

(Hélène Grenke and François Cromer, my supervisors for my third degree and first postdoc, were from France.) "Or you'll end up twisted in back pain," added the lab assistant, Leila, who had just rushed over.

Tall and lanky, Leila had worked for a long time in Professor Yossi Zlokherson's lab (where she got in through connections after being kicked out of another lab). She'd learned which rumors to pass on and which to ignore. She "knew" how to deliver the right information to the right...

How much truth was there in that "information"? Well, I'm not the one to judge...

So, they control my health as well... Wonderful!

*****

A tram appeared around the corner, its shark-like nose cutting through the air. I jumped onto the step and took a seat by the window. The man sitting opposite grunted and, almost reluctantly, stuck his tongue out at me—then dragged it unnaturally along the corner of his mouth.

I know I'm thinking the wrong thing... The tongue disappeared behind thick lips. But an unremarkable old woman in glasses, standing nearby with a prayer book, suddenly coughed sharply.

Alright, I'll think about Kainman instead...

Nedali, a Pakistani, came to Sergio Kainman's lab from France, where he had earned his third degree. He distinguished himself so much that he had to change his first and last name before coming to America. For a long time, Nedali had no results, and when Kainman licensed a grant for a lab in Memphis, he gave Nedali their project. Nedali fabricated some data; the most complex experiments were done by a Taiwanese student, who...

—Pavel German

So, the radio sums up my day... They feed me cheerful music whenever I think about the people, they want me to think about... Cheaply bought, I sank tiredly into the soft, comforting chair.

But just for fun, I decided to think about Roshti now. Barich responded, "Not in this program..."

Right, since he's connected to Yossi Zlokherson, Denver, and who knows who else... and also "digging" against Hélène Grenke, François Cromer, and possibly Nedali, though he pretends to oppose Sergio Kainman...

But how does François Cromer's or William Roshti's circle know what's happening in Kainman's lab? Spying, television, or maybe both...

I turned off the radio and pressed the red "ON" button on the TV remote. On the channel *Your News*, a political information program called *Good Evening* was airing. One of the guests claimed he knew how to achieve peace with Zelotania. He reveled in his monologues, wearing a tired, disdainful expression, rolling his eyes whenever someone disagreed with him. His arrogance and overconfidence were irritating...

Another guest tried to convince viewers that peace with Zelotania was impossible because all Zelotanians harbored a primal, innate hatred for Concordians and only understood the language of force. He looked like a naive amateur and didn't inspire trust...

Switched the TV to the *Russia channel*. On the program, *It's Healthy*, Lyudmila Malyshkina was talking about healthy eating.

"Don't drink coffee, don't eat lamb," Malyshkina urged the viewers...

I thought she must be helping some postdocs in Kainman's lab (maybe Olegik?) He used to rant that it was better to be... a sheep in a lab with a smart supervisor than a smart one in a group led by a sheep. The camera focused on Malyshkina's face as she shook her head disapprovingly, her eyes widening...

I noticed I had fallen asleep... I dreamed of Olya, the neighbor girl from our Kyiv courtyard. Suddenly, her father—an alcoholic and a troublemaker—approached and shouted right in my face!

The accusation hung heavy in the air: "You raped my daughter! Over there, in the bushes..." A new figure materialized from seemingly nowhere, a portly dwarf with a sloppily tucked-in shirt. A button at his navel was undone, revealing a protruding belly, further marred by a greasy stain at its most prominent point. He constantly darted his eyes about, as if in fear.

"What?" I roared. "I never even went on a single date with your daughter! You were warned, weren't you, you bald goat, to stay away from my family? Weren't you?!"

The "bald goat" winced, then vanished. The "witness" to the alleged rape followed close behind.

With great effort, I broke free from the grip of sleep. Even at night, it seemed, I wouldn't find peace. I remembered visiting my mother in Concordia and, while there, making a trip to the dentist, all just before my departure for Kainman's laboratory.

Even in the waiting room, I noticed a balding, Eastern-looking man with his overly tall, nearly adult daughter. He was talking to the doctor's religious secretary, who had a clump of gray hair sticking out from under her chestnut wig. The secretary suddenly blurted out:

"Your daughter is magnificent. Those who understand, understand." The secretary's words, spoken in Hebrew, hung in the air as her gaze fixed on me.

So, this is when the story with Olya began. Or perhaps even earlier, during my master's studies, when a student with the same resonant name, Olya, was a decoy in Hélène Grenke's lab. Yes, the mental hospital pursued me everywhere, from Concordia to the USA. The psychiatrists, who were also my professors, believed they understood my nature well and could manipulate me by playing on what they considered the weak strings of my psyche. But were the professors merely dancing in circles, or had they themselves become pawns in an unseen game? A game where they feared losing family, friends, jobs, social standing, and, most terrifying of all, becoming patients in a global asylum. A game in which gray eminences, hiding behind curtains, decided whose pawn would become a queen and who would burn at the stake, surrounded by idle onlookers, ubiquitous informers, and ruthless, gleeful arsonists. The public demanded new victims, and the puppeteers knew it. The guillotine, never resting, continued its work.

I woke up and decided to email Sergio Kainman, carefully asking if he thought it would be possible to assign part of the project to Dr. William Roshti. "The genetic background of these mice is so strange," I mused, "it's hard to do anything with them."

Kainman's reply came surprisingly fast, despite the ten-hour time difference. Perhaps Sergio was in Europe? He travels so much.

Kainman wrote: "Tell William Roshti to change the background of the mice, if he even gets them, that is. And why do you need this article? Your life, in any case, will never change."

> *One does not pick the passing years*
> *In them we breathe, in them we cease*
> *No vulgar plea, no bitter tears,*
> *More base than begging for release,*
>
> *As if the epochs, market-priced,*
> *Could simply be exchanged.*
> *Each age an iron grip, uniced,*
> *Yet where a wondrous garden's ranged,*
> *A single cloud, ablaze.*
>
> *A firm, close embrace.*
> *Time is skin, not a dress.*
> *Its imprint runs deep.*
> *Like fingerprints on fingertips,*
> *Time leaves its lines and folds on us—*
> *If you look closely, you can read them.*
>
> *—Alexander Kushner*

I Want the Grail

King Philip IV usually awoke at dawn, but today he rose later than usual. He was tormented by weakness, a runny nose, and a fever—likely picked up during the hunt.

"Chico, where are you?" he called to his servant. "Chico, how long must I wait? Where are you, you old rogue?"

The door creaked open, and Chico tiptoed in. He was old, hunched, and silver-haired, but had served his master with unwavering loyalty. In his hands, he carried a jug of warm water and a towel.

"You'd have done better to bring me some medicine..." Philip sneezed loudly.

"Sire, I daresay the Holy Grail of Monsieur de Molay would cure you at once."

"The Grail? Does it truly exist?"

"They say it does, just as they speak of the vast treasures of the Templar Order."

"The Order... de Molay... How much longer must I hear about them? My kingdom is drowning in debt, yet that de Molay dares mock me. Listen, Chico—I want the Grail."

"But the Templars obtained it through honorable struggle..."

"Perhaps you didn't hear me clearly. If the King of France desires something, he shall have it—without exception. Send Kleber to me."

"You summoned me, Your Majesty?"

Kleber stood frozen in a deep bow. He had been eavesdropping just outside the door, and the moment the King spoke his name, he stepped forward to appear before Philip IV.

Kleber hesitated... Which path should he take? Never before had he faced such a powerful adversary. For this reason, he needed the king's counsel.

"There are two scoundrels—members of the Templar Order—Skin de Florian and Noffo Dei," Kleber said cautiously. "They're mired in debt and willing to offer any assistance to His Majesty..."

"What do I care about them?" Philip grimaced. "I want the Grail—and a confession from the Templar leadership of their shameful crimes."

"Of course, Your Majesty," Kleber replied, bowing deeply.

"Go."

"A good day to you, Your Majesty..."

Miscellaneous

The lowered blinds kept the sunlight from breaking into the room. In the dimness, one could find a sense of calm and focus on the things truly worth thinking about...

Earlier today, on the city bus, I had a run-in with an elderly man who sat next to me. I had asked a Russian-speaking couple nearby, in Russian, *"What time is it?"* The old man didn't take long to react:

"They've swarmed in. Ruined our country..."

"Your country is a cesspool of hypocrites and ignorant brutes," the young woman snapped back.

"Bandits! Pimps! Racketeers! Go back to wherever you came from!" the old man ranted on. The girl shrugged, seemingly about to respond, but I was no longer listening... In haste, I got off at the nearest stop, leaving all three of them behind in the epicenter of their "fascinating" debate.

When I arrived at work, more unpleasant surprises were waiting for me. The electrophoresis didn't work, again. It had already been three weeks of the same. I had changed the reagents. I'd even borrowed fresh solutions from another lab. All in vain.

Only William Roshti, smirking as always, asked: "So, how are your experiments going? Got any new results?"

And Zlocherson, walking past me, melted into a grin: "How's it going, Volodya?"

He stuffed his hands into the back pockets of his pants, clearly mimicking our lab supervisor, Jacqueline, who once, quite unabashedly, slipped her right hand into the left back pocket of my trousers...

Using a "proven" method of combating sabotage, I've been sitting at the lab bench for two days straight, hoping to get at least *some* kind of result from an experiment. In the end, I can't take it anymore; I lower my head and fall asleep.

I dream that I'm in medieval France...

I'm galloping across a stone bridge toward the open gates of a castle. My cloak flutters wildly in the wind. My cheeks burn, perhaps from the cold, perhaps from the chase. I lash my horse without mercy; the fate of the Templar Order depends on my mission.

In a tower window, a candle burns. I'm expected. But the king's men are right on my heels. I turn and fire a bolt from my crossbow. One of the pursuers, pierced through, falls from his horse. Someone catches up and swings a sword at me.

I draw my own blade, block the strike, and counterattack. The man slumps from his saddle with barely a cry...

Suddenly, Lisitsky charges toward me, clad in armor, mounted on a horse patched with metal plates, lance at the ready.

"Death to the Templars!" Lisitsky roars.

"Long live de Molay!" I shout back.

Without slowing my horse, at full gallop, I leap onto the saddle of one of the pursuers.

Throwing the rider off, I seize his lance.

And so, Lisitsky and I charge toward each other, consumed with the obsession to destroy our enemy.

But what's this? A treacherous arrow pierces my hand...

I have no strength left to strike Lisitsky with my lance...

Yet we collide anyway.

Our lances shatter, and, still in our saddles, we ride away from each other...

Before I could fully react, they caught up to me and pressed a dagger to my throat, painfully twisting my wounded arm.

But my horse dragged me toward the ruins of an old building.

I burst through a half-built wooden wall into a basement room, shielding my face with my hands.

A beam collapsed onto my shoulders. I fell from the horse, rolling and sprawling across the floor.

They grabbed me tightly, but then stood me up, dusted me off, loosened their grip, and handed me a sword.

In the far corner of the room stood a ladder.

On it, Jacqueline was tied up, gagged.

"Come on," the captain of the guard commanded impatiently.

I took a step toward the ladder, but in an instant, I spun around and plunged the sword into the chest of the guard who hadn't even registered what was happening...

The scene shifts in an instant—like a kaleidoscope twisting through shards of reality.

I stand shirtless on the rooftop of a towering skyscraper, the wind from the helicopter's spinning blades biting into my bare skin.

Inside the hovering craft, William Roshti and lab assistant Tatiana sit, armored in bulletproof vests and helmets. Their cold, unblinking eyes lock onto me, unyielding and unreadable.

"You made a mistake," Rochti snarls through clenched teeth.

The helicopter surges upward, rising into the sky, shrinking to a speck, then vanishing entirely into the cloudless blue.

I jolt awake. My head pounds, a relentless ringing echoing in my ears.

Dragging myself to the sink, I fill a glass with water and drink it down in one desperate gulp, wiping my mouth with the sleeve of my shirt.

The day awaits, heavy with uncertainty.

******

The long day was fading away in a blazing sunset. The sun still lit torn fragments of the sky, but a cool, velvet night was taking hold, darkening most of the heavens, except for a rosy horizon glowing in the west. A broad-shouldered, lean psychologist, maybe a psychotherapist, I'm not sure, fixed me with a steady gaze, his well-toned arm propped on the chair.

"Have you thought about ending it all?" he asked.

Not the first time I'd heard that question.

"No, I haven't," I said, forcing a bright voice that barely masked the emptiness.

The next day, William Roshti was mocking me, flicking a ballpoint pen between his fingers.

"How's your mood? Thinking of seeing a shrink? You've got to be honest with them..."

"You promised me this would end someday. Isn't that right?" I shot back, desperation leaking into my voice.

"Alright," the psychologist said hesitantly. "It all depends on the situation in the country and the world. For now, continue taking the medication I prescribed."

"What does the state of the country have to do with any of this? All I want is to live a normal life, like everyone else."

"I warned you to quit that project. You're a stubborn narcissist," the psychologist said, eyes sharp. "If something goes wrong, at work or at home—you'd better come straight to me."

I wanted to argue, to fight back, but invisible chains gripped me tight. My whole body trembled, and against every fiber of my will, the word slipped out: *"Absolutely."*

That very night, the word haunted me. It echoed endlessly on the Russian-language radio, sometimes fitting, sometimes not. The host, Tatiana Barich, kept repeating it in every broadcast, like a stubborn refrain: *"Absolutely..."*

"Take your medication," the psychologist insisted.

"Is there no way without them?" I asked, desperation creeping into my voice.

"No. Without those pills, you'll feel like you're falling apart."

I already knew the truth. The one time I forgot to take them, every step felt like a drum pounding inside my skull. My head spun uncontrollably one moment, then throbbed with unbearable pain the next.

Had they really hooked me on these drugs like a junkie on a needle? Was this to be my sentence for the rest of my life?

At home, the nightmare that was my neighbor Shuli raged on. She methodically scattered marbles across the floor, their sharp clatter echoing in the silence like nails on a chalkboard, driving me slowly mad. Shuli had never been easy, but ever since my mother moved in, she had become relentless.

The moment my mother settled into the building, Shuli stormed over, arms flailing, shouting her protests against the renovations in my mother's apartment and even the rightful use of the parking space. She had gone so far as to disable the elevator to stop the workers from hauling materials upstairs.

Then came the flooding, Shuli's doing. Water spilled into our apartment, and the plaster cracked and peeled, while mold began to creep across the ceiling and walls. Yet Shuli refused to pay for a single repair.

I wanted to call a lawyer, to fight back, but my mother hushed me sharply. "Don't get involved with criminals," she warned. "Shuli's threatened to rob us, and the police? They won't find a thing."

Somehow, I fell asleep that night. But it was a cruel rest.

I jolted awake, drenched in sweat, after a terrifying dream. In it, a burly man in a white coat was brutally twisting my genitals. Every muscle in my body tensed as I tried to push away, to escape the nightmare, but I could barely move...

I barely managed to lift my head for a moment before it fell back helplessly onto the pillow. My arms, no longer under my control, hung off the bed like whips.

Taking a pair of garden shears, the so-called "orderly" cut off my penis and threw it to the floor.

"Let's see if you can get an erection now," he sneered, laughing, his mouth wide open, revealing gold teeth.

Even after waking, I felt the sharp pain and heard that unbearable voice. I could have sworn it was coming from Concordia Radio long before I left for America...

Outside, a full moon shone, split in two by storm clouds. On a hill blanketed with pine trees, a lone wolf howled.

Behind the wall, my mother coughed. The doctors suspected pneumonia.

A woman who knew my mother, an agent placed by the security services, grabbed my arm and warned me:

"Your mother will keep falling ill if you continue talking about Sergio Kainman. Now you see what kind of people support Kainman... The only question left is who's sending..."

Unpleasant dreams haunted my nights, but the waking world was no refuge. It felt as though the factions, once split into opposing teams, had secretly banded together, united against me and my family.

The signs were impossible to ignore. Certain branches of the intelligence services seemed to be backing Kainman, weaving a web of deceit and disinformation that tangled us all. They were orchestrating a campaign not just against me, but against everything I stood for.

The psychologist, recommended by that mysterious woman connected to my mother, had warned me in no uncertain terms: *"You'll break out in herpes. Your electrical appliances at home will malfunction repeatedly. All because you speak too freely."*

His voice had dropped suddenly, the words slicing through the silence like a knife: *"Not yet. If your former mentor sends you those two words, it means the article won't be published anywhere."*

I had no choice but to dwell on that phrase.

Just the day before, an email from Sergio had arrived—a brief reply to my urgent question: Had Kainman seen my manuscript?

"Not yet."

Those two words echoed in my mind like a cryptic warning. The battle was far from over, and the forces aligned against me were playing a dangerous game, one I was only beginning to understand.

Every shadow felt heavier, every whisper more threatening. The walls closed in, and I knew that the truth I sought might come at a terrible price.

In the dull, abandoned scribbles,
I sought my breath, my refuge true.
In long, oppressive evenings' grip,
I tried to cheat my fate anew.

But fate cannot be fooled or bent.
The fallen leaves in whisper sigh.
Amid the sunset's fiery blaze,
A light shines from my window high.

So, this, it seems, must be my road:
With stones displaced, and icy streams,
A chilling dread within my chest
As broken as my shattered dreams.

And clashing heads upon the stage
Must I decide my enemy?

I took a sleeping pill and finally fell asleep at dawn. In my dream, the young man from Kainman's lab was conducting a harsh interrogation...

"Where's the plasmid you stole from Sergio Kainman?"

"I don't know... probably in the old, dilapidated garage..." I blurted out, twisting my stiff arms bound behind the chair.

"The garage, near the house?" the police officer sitting on the table, his pistol hanging from his belt, jumped into the conversation. "You bastard, don't dodge the question. We'll find the plasmid anyway and drag you out into the light..."

Kainman's student calmly placed a hand on the officer's shoulder, then leaned back in his chair and continued: "Volodya, we don't wish you harm, believe me. Just tell us where the plasmid is, and we'll let you go..."

He lit a cigarette, exhaled a plume of smoke, swayed slightly in the chair, and added, "And one more thing, and the second."

"The signaling complex on the mitochondrial membrane... Tell us about it," he said, leaning forward, locking eyes with me as he blew cigarette smoke right in my face.

Gripping the ends of the ropes binding my wrists, I managed to free myself. I lunged toward the table and grabbed a letter opener lying there. But the policeman drew a black pistol that had been hanging idle at his side and fired at me point-blank...

At that moment, I snapped fully awake, lying on the floor, shielding my face with scattered notes.

I had no idea what garage they were talking about. Neither in Kyiv, nor Concordia, nor America did I, or my parents, own any garage.

And all the plasmids and cells? I had handed them over to Kainman's lab assistant six months before leaving...

The sun was already high, casting uneven light across the streets. It spilled down tiled roofs onto the sidewalks and knocked on windows, beckoning the sleepy residents outside.

Time to get dressed and go to work.

Flicker, flicker, people all around,
I move along, and somehow, it's comforting—

Like Ulysses, I drive myself onward,
Yet still, I'm moving backward as before.

—Joseph Brodsky

The Fall of Acre

The year was 1291 AD. The Crusaders' fortunes had markedly declined. In fact, they had been expelled from almost all of the Holy Land, their only remaining stronghold being the fortress city of Acre.

The Siege of Acre stands as a poignant symbol of the Crusades themselves, a reflection of both their valor and their failures.

A protracted series of betrayals by the monarchs of Aragon and Sicily, along with the Genoese, who were principal defenders of Tripoli and had forged a defensive alliance with the Egyptian Sultan Al-Ashraf Khalil (known in the West as Qalawun's successor), further eroded Crusader resistance. King Henry II of Cyprus and Jerusalem's abrupt flight from Acre to Cyprus with his forces underscored the disarray. Moreover, internal treachery within the ranks of the Knights Templar compounded the crisis.

The military orders, the Hospitallers, Templars, and Teutonic Knights, answered solely to their own commanders, while the secular forces, led by Henry II, the King of Cyprus and Jerusalem, operated under a fragmented command. This lack of unified leadership critically undermined the Crusader defense.

Henry II bore the full title of King of Cyprus and Jerusalem, though Jerusalem had long since ceased to be part of his kingdom. Despite the honorific, his claim to the Holy City was purely titular, reflecting the Crusaders' diminished hold over the region. Moreover, the heavily armored knights, who excelled in open-field battles like fish in water, were ill-suited for the confined and treacherous combat on fortress walls and within city streets.

Credit must be given to Sultan Qalawun. In a remarkably short time, he assembled a highly effective army and transported it from Egypt to the walls of Acre, catching the Crusaders completely off guard.

However, Qalawun himself did not live to fulfill his promise to expel the infidels from the entirety of the Holy Land; he died en route. His son, Al-Malik al-Ashraf Khalil, inherited his cause and proved equally relentless against the Christian adversaries.

Repeatedly, the Mamluks, effectively employing battering engines, broke through the ruined outer wall and pushed deep into the city. However, each time the defenders, through extraordinary effort and sacrifice, managed to repel them beyond the fortress walls.

Emboldened by these victories, the Crusaders launched several successful sorties.

De Molay participated in every Templar attack. Now, he rode at the right hand of the Grand Master of the Order. In the enemy's tents, his horse became entangled in ropes, and De Molay was unable to continue the charge...

Nevertheless, with mighty swings of his sword, he cut down two Mamluks.

The sortie ended in failure. An arrow fired from the fortress served as a warning to the besiegers, they were ready. Many knights were captured and later executed by beheading.

Only after returning to the fortress did De Molay learn of the Grand Master's death. An arrow had pierced his side, and as he fell from his horse, he whispered, "My God, I am slain. What will become of Acre?"

De Molay was immediately recommended for the position of Grand Master of the Order.

"He has a tendency to seek unconventional solutions," some said.

"He is harsh in his judgments. He lacks the talent of a diplomat, which is so necessary for negotiations with the Pope and the rulers of Europe," others argued.

"He is bold and assertive," replied those who passionately supported De Molay. And they won.

De Molay became the Grand Master of the Knights Templar. The last Grand Master... He was also the last to lead the Order in battles in the Holy Land. Shortly before the fall of Acre, De Molay evacuated to Cyprus along with the Order's treasury. He was one of the last to leave the abandoned city.

Ladies

How could I possibly cope with the overwhelming number of girls who were practically throwing themselves at me during my final postdoctoral year with Kahneman?

The girl attack began the moment it became clear I was leaving…

The girls would introduce themselves without prompting, while standing with me in line at the cafeteria, on the way home, in the parking lot, or ambushing me outside the building where I worked… Bold ones.

The cafeteria servers and supermarket cashiers often tried to strike up conversations, sometimes even hinting at going on a date.

“Excuse me… do you know where the bus stop is?”
“No,” I said, deliberately not telling the truth, just to be cautious.
“I’m new in town. I don’t know anyone in San Francisco… maybe we could grab a coffee sometime?”
“Not today. But I can give you my cell number.”

There was another time when Olezhek invited me for coffee. While we were in line at the cafeteria, he stood ahead of me and gave a subtle nod to the girl behind the counter, as if to say, “That’s him.” Later, that same girl, in her straightforward way, confided in me and asked, "Could you help me find a job?" I mentioned it to Olezhek... and he got so worked up he nearly broke the pipette he was holding. "What a fool," he snapped.

Most of the time, I either remained completely indifferent or, when someone was particularly persistent, gave them my phone number, without asking for theirs.

But indifference, as I came to learn, can be a serious offense to some women.

And one of them filed a complaint.

I was called into the office and subjected to a moral lecture, as they carefully watched my reaction.

"What if we told your boss?" someone said.

I let the question slide and began to defend myself.

"Well, first of all, we went on a date."

"Once," and a perfectly sharpened pencil, as if extending the official's index finger, shot upward beside her temple.

"Yes, but a few days later, she gave me her cell phone number..."

"And then?"

"Then, about a week later, seeing that nothing was progressing, I wrote her a letter and ended it with: 'I *wish you only the best. Goodbye.*'

"A few days after that, Janet, that was her name, sent me an email. Mind you, I had never given her my email address... I replied, and from there, a correspondence began between us."

"I want to see those emails," someone interrupted.

I ignored that as well... and continued.

"Several times in my messages, I asked her, '*How many times do I have to write to you: I wish you only the best?*' But she kept writing to me..."

The pencil slipped from her hand, hit the desk, and rolled onto the floor. But I hadn't delivered my final blow just yet.

"I hadn't spoken to Janet for two months. So why did she suddenly call me?" I held up my phone, showing her number listed in the incoming calls.

"By accident? That's too many coincidences... I'm ready to defend myself in any setting, even if it means hiring a lawyer." With those words, I stood up and walked out of the office.

The match had been decided in the first half.

I kept reflecting on the whole story... how Janet had flirted with me in front of others, witnesses who, for some reason, always turned their heads away, avoiding eye contact with her. I remembered Hans and the South Korean postdoc, Park, who worked with Antoshka on a joint project. They both surely knew something...

What a mess, huh? The way she used me, especially when I was running FACS experiments for her...

But just then, Zlocherson approached and gripped my hand firmly in anger, pulling me back down to earth.

However, I remembered the fortune-teller Margalit, the one I was introduced to by tall Lily. Yes, the same Lily who used to work for Zlocherson.

Margalit had told me that at Kahneman's lab, I would end up working with a "smart" Pakistani and get involved with a mysterious girl from Europe. She also gave me a few superficial details that matched Janet's profile... but I'll leave those out.

In short, this was a planned operation, orchestrated by Zlocherson and his "friends."

The "smart" Pakistani had been provoking me for four years and actively sabotaging my work, pouring filth into my cages, convincing the lab assistant not to do genotyping on my mice... inciting others against me...

He also turned other postdocs and Jacqueline against me...

Moreover, he stole my ideas, passing them off as his own, eavesdropped on my conversations with other postdocs, peeked over my shoulder at my graphs on the computer, graphs I hadn't yet presented at lab meetings, or directly asked for my advice on his project (these conversations he kept secret).

Nedali was close friends with Hans, and both of them would hover around my workspace for days on end, tormented by boredom, uselessness, and resentment.

The "clairvoyant" either didn't know or didn't want to know about any of this... She merely said, with either sadness or frustration, apparently having heard this from someone else: "Well, since you have the fellowship, just work."

My hand slipped out of Zlocherson's grasp, and he quickly disappeared into his laboratory.

During those days of unimaginable encounters, I often found myself thinking about Amy. If it had been possible, I would have crawled all the way from California to Boston... Perhaps I was pitying myself, because deep down I knew we were never meant to be together for life, even if we had both stayed in Denver. Feelings born out of self-pity can be anything but love.

So, back in my distant youth in Kyiv, I met a girl who seemed to share my pride. Golden autumn hid itself in her long, loose, light-brown hair. Her small, firm breasts stirred confusion in my fragile, post-adolescent thoughts.

"Look, learn everything," she said, smiling as she handed me her lecture notes, as a top student.

And I... I was afraid. I was neither a top student nor an alpha male, nor a macho. My pride was crushed by my own cowardice, which revealed to me my true, unenviable place, beside pretty, but not very bright and self-absorbed women...

Life was just beginning, but I was crushed to the ground under the weight of a relentless sentence. I wanted something different, but I was unworthy, and I no longer encountered that "something different."

Chance comes rarely in life, and happy is the one who seizes it...

And don't tell me, "Everything happens for the best," that's empty nonsense for... for complete losers. Life is like a wild mustang that you have to learn to tame. And for that, you don't necessarily need to be an alpha male, a macho, or even a top student.

Perhaps the main takeaway from my American experience is a sense of reality. Only, it came to me far too late.

> *Along the Smolensk Road, the blizzard bites my face,*
> *Life's relentless duties chase me from my place.*
> *If only your ring were stronger on your hand,*
> *The journey might feel shorter across this land.*
>
> *Along the Smolensk Road, the forests stretch and sway,*
> *Along the Smolensk Road, the power lines hum away.*

—Bulat Okudzhava

As for Olezhek... This man was undermining me, perhaps not as blatantly as Nedali... But in my final year at Kahneman's lab, he decided he could reap some decent benefits from my departure. Olezhek called it a "winning situation."

"Listen, old man," he said, "my wife got a position in the lab where there's a 'winning situation.' The postdoc left the lab and abandoned a project. My wife will continue that project and publish it quickly."

Yes, Olezhek kept his large, potato-shaped nose to the wind and knew how to survive in our "rapid response squad." Like Nedali, he used Lisitsky's and Zlocherson's lies to persecute me in the lab. Like Nedali, he was an informant, a racketeer, and a pimp. Like Nedali, he had the support of television...

Only Nedali had his people in the student union.

But Olezhek was eavesdropping on my private phone conversations at home... an unusual role for a postdoc.

Well, Olezhek couldn't resist grabbing a piece of the pie if it was right there on the table... If the Swiss professor (a luminary in immunology who recently passed away from a heart attack at a ski resort) could take the bulk of my second project from generous hands, without asking me or giving me anything in return, yet the Swiss professor's paper got published in *Nature* magazine, "Well, why shouldn't Olezhek be allowed to do the same?"

"Volodya, let's go grab some coffee," he suggested. I agreed, and we headed to the cafeteria located by the university library.

As I half-listened to Olezhek's constant murmuring, my attention was caught by a book standing upright on a shelf. Its title read "*Spartak*, *The People's Team*."

What a coincidence: Olezhek was also a fan of Spartak... I shifted my gaze from the bookshelf to Olezhek and back again. I was surprised to see a Russian-language book so prominently displayed in an American library.

It reminded me of a match in Moscow. The club *Dynamo Kyiv* was playing against one of the Moscow teams. The TV announcer, barely hiding his sympathies, nearly shouted into the microphone: "Journalists, photographers, and fans gathered behind the Kyiv Dynamo goal, all waiting for a goal..."

But they didn't get one. Kyiv won the match.

Olezhek tried some of his dirty tricks. He complained to Jacqueline that I refused to work with him and that I had the audacity to plan experiments on

TH-17 lymphocytes, his so-called "untouchable territory."

"You're messing with our people," he said.

He also attempted to blackmail me by threatening to withhold mice, for I'll add that Olezhek wasn't entirely to blame: after all, I behaved childishly in a game that was anything but child's play... In the end, he warned me it would be better to fly home to Concordia, not from San Francisco, but from Los Angeles. I wonder how he knew that?

Unfortunately, I didn't listen to him back then... and I regret it. The flight was anything but ordinary. Strange people circled around me... They asked strange questions... Flirtatious flight attendants and fellow passengers fussed about...

Unintentionally, I glanced back and locked eyes with a man who looked just like one of my psychologists from Concordia.

That's when I took a postcard showing an airline plane pierced by a rod... These postcards, with Velcro backs, were handed out by the attentive flight attendants. Turning the postcard in my hands, I stuck it upside down to the back of the seat in front of me, on the edge, so it could be seen from behind. It looked like a penis with petals...

Then I closed my eyes and pretended to sleep, until I actually did.

When I woke up, I discovered that my carry-on had been rummaged through, my baggage claim ticket had been dropped onto the airplane floor, and my passport had been taken. This was the second time I'd lost my passport within six months.

Upon arriving in Concordia, I reported the incident to the police. A slender, smiling policewoman disappeared for a while, then reappeared holding my passport.
"Stick close to the Concordians," she advised me.

Easy to say... But I never wanted to know Concordians like the vile trickster Lisitsky. From early childhood, he was into numismatics, buying expensive ancient coins with money of unclear origin. When Lisitsky enrolled to study pharmacy, he picked up new hobbies. He wandered from pub to pub looking for drinks, available girls, and juicy gossip, which he later relayed to whoever needed to hear it.

He was probably an informant from birth, and many things were forgiven him. For four consecutive years, Lisitsky cheated on his university exams... yet somehow managed to earn his pharmacist's license in the end.

He taught the Concordian language to underage immigrant girls and, abusing his position, slept with some of them... (He even tried to set one of them up with me).

Having indulged in earthly pleasures, Lisitsky...

He started using heroin... He often told his patrons blatant lies about his drinking buddies. Hatred and inadequacy, selfishness and envy, all these drove Lisitsky. He couldn't forgive those who had earned a third degree because he himself was expelled for poor performance after the second.

He remembered the slightest offenses and took revenge on everyone with a stable personal life... Angelina Pustovoitova married another man, not him...

I made the mistake of running into her at a café, and, on top of that, I was preparing to leave for a postdoc in America. I brought a souvenir from America for our mutual acquaintance, but not for Lisitsky.

I told Lisitsky that I liked the music from the movie *"At Home Among Strangers"*.

And just like that, the narrow-minded informers surrounding me on campus started whispering about my unreliability...

Who knows what could have come into Lisitsky's fevered mind... And he held no forgiveness, neither for me nor for Angelina. His brazen lies spread throughout the campus and eventually followed me to America.

Zlocherson was just waiting for a chance to get revenge on me for leaving him for Grenke's lab.

And, of course, both of them gained something from spreading those lies.

Lisitsky did everything fast. He devoured shawarma quickly, briefly satisfying his eternally insatiable appetite before heading to the bar. He cheated on exams and tests swiftly, with the help of his former girlfriend. He dumped her quickly when the time came to choose. And he ratted out others fast whenever he could gain dividends or cover his own mistakes.

Who in San Francisco? Is it even worth listing all my so-called well-wishers... Lisitsky found Zlocherson, and Zlocherson found Lisitsky. Zlocherson knew how to "sell dossiers" on students or even professors. Having skillfully handed over a fabricated "compromising dossier" on me to Denver, Zlocherson could comfortably step back, knowing the "file" would follow me everywhere in America, and beyond.

He cruised the university campus in his brand-new Lexus SUV, well beyond a professor's salary, making it clear to everyone: you can fabricate a case against anyone.

Meanwhile, Sergio Kainman threw dozens of such "dossiers," with their implicated parties, into the turbulent river of lab life and watched who would survive and who wouldn't. Sometimes, when Kahneman's and the postdoc's interests aligned, the "kind" Kahneman would toss a lifeline for a while... And sometimes, he'd hit you over the head with an oar.

During my final visit to San Francisco, I met with Professor Kahneman at a Mexican eatery (I still miss those hefty burritos paired with dark beer). Throughout our conversation, he was evasive. Kahneman had no intention of lifting a finger to publish my work.

"Do you recognize this place?" he warned me at the start of our talk.

How could I not? I spent two days hugging the toilet...

But I wasn't poisoned here, instead, it happened at the cafeteria I visited after lunch at that eatery. All because I was supposedly (!) connected to those who filed complaints to scientific journals accusing Kahneman of fabricating articles...

It was a shameless denunciation, woven from dirty threads by Olezhek and Antoshka! Kahneman, of course, knew this, but even here, he outdid himself. He tried to silence me and, at the same time, turn me against the Latin American community.

I needed to say something immediately... But what? My mind was spinning with a meaningless, unhelpful, chaotic mosaic that kept me from focusing...

Here I am on a pedal boat with my father... I dive into the water... No, that's not it...

Now I'm holding a flapping flounder by the gills and shouting to my father to come...

I needed help. No, that's not it...

I enrolled in medical school on August 1st. Three years later, on August 1st, I returned to Kyiv... Two years after that, on the first day of the eighth month, I visited Jerusalem for the first time... I was born in 1970... On August 1st of that year, Otto Warburg died...

Stop! "The Warburg effect"!"You can't study cancer in these mice due to the disrupted pentose phosphate shunt," I croaked out.

Kahneman, who had started to rise, sat back down. He reached into his pocket for a handkerchief to wipe the sweat forming on his brow...

At the neighboring table, there was loud applause.

Olezhek's project, like the Titanic striking a floating iceberg, was sinking fast...

The little man in the black tailcoat fulfilled his promise. He transported me two years into the future... But I was not happy about it.

The orange hue so draws us near,
It blocks our path, it fuels our fear.
Surrendered to its glowing light,
Our bodies melt and lose their might.

Yet still we fan the blazing fire,
Drawn deeper in its fierce desire.
Once more we risk ourselves, unknown,
Entrusting flames to take their throne.

Our fate remains unseen, concealed,
Within the smoke yet unrevealed.
Will we emerge, alive and free,
Or in the fire cease to be?

—Bella Akhmadulina

The End

And yet, they agreed. They agreed that the investigation, initiated by the king, would examine the order's activities, audit their accounts, interrogate their members, and even the grand master himself.

Umberto Eco writes that the Templars, like all Crusaders, were madmen... Indeed, only the mad could have agreed to such an extensive investigation into their affairs. Were they truly so confident in their innocence or in the fairness of the court? Or perhaps the Templars simply had no other choice. Try saying "No" to a monarch...

They only delayed their doom but could not escape it.

At first, the investigators behaved with studied politeness. But very soon, pleas and requests gave way to the rack and the iron maiden...

Years passed, and some did not withstand the torture and blackmail... But the grand master remained steadfast and unyielding.

Moreover, there was no clarity about the location of the treasures, and most importantly—the Holy Grail.

Kleber worked "to the sweat of his brow." He personally participated in interrogations and tortures, shuttling between the prison and the king's palace, keeping Philip informed of everything.

He even resorted to cunning—he hid the Templars' account records and then declared that the Templars refused to account for their usury and cooperate with the investigation...

At last, the king grew weary...

Kleber, you've been struggling with these filthy Templars for five years... Five years, and you're testing my patience. "Your Majesty, they are aided by unclean forces..."

"And you are aided by the King of France himself, the anointed of God... Where is the gold? Where is the Grail? Where are the confessions of De Molay and his circle?"

"Your Majesty, I need more time..."

"I tell you, you have none. Order the burning of these heretics. We have enough evidence. Of course, it would be best if all the Templars sailed off on a Crusade and never returned... 'By the hand of the enemy, the enemy falls,'" Philip mused aloud. "We need the blessing of that old fool Clement, and then we will rally all the knights with a call to free the Holy Sepulcher from the hands of the infidels."

"But where will we find the money? The Templars are in prison; the Jews and Lombards have hidden away in their burrows and transferred all the funds abroad... No, we have no way out, and no time either..."

When De Molay was brought word of his execution, he sat on a donkey. For the umpteenth time, the jailers had laced his food with various potions... At times, tears would flow without reason, and he felt an unbearable urge to break free from the choking smoke rising from what was called the chimney (but was simply a smoke shaft). He tried in vain to...

He tried to break the prison bars and, in despair, tore at his clothes. Often, unbearable weakness would wash over his entire body, especially his legs, right after eating, and he would collapse exhausted onto the hay. The jailers shouted from behind the doors, "Sir De Molay, you need to rest... Go to your estate."

Sometimes, upon waking, he suffered unbearable itching in his legs. Apparently, something was being slipped into his cell while he walked in the prison yard... Eventually, he was simply poisoned.

Within two days, he vomited all over the cell.

Now, in a way, De Molay felt relief... An end to torture, an end to interrogations, an end to suffering...

They were tied to stakes amid the dry wooden planks... Executioners stood before them, holding burning torches. The archbishop read the sentence. The Templars did not listen... Soon, very soon, they would find eternal bliss. They sang...

"Not unto us, O Lord, not unto us, but to Your name give glory..."

Philip waved his handkerchief. Kleber gave the order, and the torches ignited the fire. De Molay choked on the smoke; tongues of flame licked his body, burning him...

Philip waved his handkerchief. Kleber gave the order, and the torches ignited the fire. De Molay choked on the smoke; tongues of flame lickeds his body, burning him...

"And yet," he shouted a curse upon the king and his entire dynasty.

They say the remaining little finger, still wearing a ring, served as a grim reminder of that curse... Whether true or not, King Philip IV died that very year, and soon after, the Capetian dynasty came to an end. All three of the king's sons mysteriously passed away, leaving no heir to the throne...

Epilogue

The drone flew low over the shopping center. Blocking out the sun, it drew closer to its own shadow. Suddenly, small, dazzling sparks appeared beneath its wings, followed immediately by a deafening crack. Many people dropped instantly. Others began to scatter wildly across the plaza, like frightened mice trapped in a cage...

I ran with the crowd but stumbled and fell. Next to me lay a dead guard. I reached out and pulled his pistol from the holster. It was relatively easy, the holster was still fastened by only one rivet. Meanwhile, the drone flew away...

The news reported a failed military coup. Many officers, high-ranking military officials, and politicians had been detained and were already giving testimony... The Prime Minister ordered a state of emergency. The constitution and freedom of the press were suspended...

I was walking across the university campus, hiding a pistol against my chest. At the doors of the pharmacy school stood several police officers. One of them, seeing me trembling as I poorly concealed the weapon, aimed and fired. The bullet struck my shoulder. Crying out from the sudden, sharp pain, I ran. The police tried to pursue me, but I managed to disappear for a while...

And now, I sit on the sandy shore of a lake with a hastily made bandage, waiting...

Here, I should rewrite the ending of Umberto Eco's novel *Foucault's Pendulum*, the world is so green, the water unnaturally clear and blue, and... it's a good place to wait for "them" to come for me...

And indeed, nearby in the village, several police cars with flashing lights appeared. Armed men in police uniforms got out. They began combing the neighborhood, house by house.

And so, it was the end. Just a little longer to wait... That was the last thought in my mind.

I turned the pistol's barrel to my temple and pulled the trigger. A misfire! I tried again, but the gun clicked empty once more. Frustrated, I threw it aside, no longer needed.

Now there was nothing left but to wait, humming some melody under my breath to chase away the unwanted thoughts...

Then something unimaginable happened—the pain, the weight, the anxiety in my chest over a shattered life, an unpublished article, the fear that someone might plagiarize it, the public reading of my thoughts, and everything happening around me, all of it vanished.

As if a kind angel had touched me with an invisible, divine hand. No longer did sweet-talking liars or rude fools trouble me.

I felt a joy so pure, it was only ever known in childhood.

I stopped being afraid.

The Templars (French: Templars—"Knights of the Temple"), also known by their official names as the Order of the Poor Knights of Christ (French: L'Ordre des Pauvres Chevaliers du Christ), the Order of the Poor Knights of the Temple of Jerusalem (French: L'Ordre des Pauvres Chevaliers du Temple de Jerusalem), and the Poor Soldiers of Christ and of the Temple of Solomon (Latin: Pauperes commilitones Christi Templique Solomonic), were a religious-military order founded in the Holy Land in 1119 by a small group of knights led by Hugh de Payens after the First Crusade. They were the second military religious order to be established (after the Hospitallers).

In the 12th and 13th centuries, the Order was extremely wealthy, owning vast landholdings both in the Crusader states established in Palestine and Syria, and across Europe. The Order also enjoyed extensive ecclesiastical and legal privileges granted by the Pope, to whom it was directly subordinate, as well as by monarchs of the lands where it held estates and properties.

The Order often fulfilled military defense roles for the Crusader states in the East, although its primary declared purpose at its founding was to protect pilgrims traveling to the Holy Land.

In 1291, when the Crusaders were expelled from Palestine by the Egyptian Sultan Khalil al-Ashraf, the Templars shifted their focus to moneylending and trade, accumulating...

They accumulated significant wealth and found themselves entangled in complex financial and property disputes with the kings of European states and the Pope.

Between 1307 and 1314, members of the Order were arrested, tortured, and executed by order of the French king Philip IV, powerful feudal lords, and the Roman Catholic Church. As a result, the Order was officially dissolved by Pope Clement V in 1312.

Source: Wikipedia, The Free Encyclopedia

The past has long been barred to me,
And what use is the past now?
What's there?—Bloodstained stones,
Or a sealed door,
Or an echo that still can't
Be silenced, though I beg it...
The same has happened to this echo
As to what I carry in my heart.
—Anna Akhmatova

PART 2

I. Chronicles of "Another Place."

"*A shady place,*" Dimas said, pointing to a star falling over the city. I hesitated and didn't get a chance to make a wish. That's always how it goes, either I don't make wishes when I should... or when I do, in a quiet half-whisper, the opposite ends up happening.

"You're going to start working at a new spot," Dimas rasped, clearing his throat. "In a big family, don't be flapping your gums," and then he burst out laughing with his ominous chuckle.

Dimas considered himself someone who understood human nature, because he was very sociable and, by his own account, had life experience, though he often told me he was an outsider. Apparently, he thought this would help him gain my trust.

"I'll try," I answered, playing along.

"Sure, this isn't America... Hmm... But unlike America, there are plenty of places here where history just breathes on you."

"Well, America has its charms too. The nature in the national parks is stunning, and not just there." (I remembered the snowy mountain peaks and the rushing forest stream where patient fishermen stood waist-deep in cold water on the way to Yellowstone.)

"Yeah, nature..." He looked down for a moment and then continued, "Look, be ready, there's a lot of talk at the Academy..." Dimas laughed again, wiping tears from his eyes. "And don't get involved with the 'all-powerful' Zlokherson. He's already got a grudge against you..."

But I had no time for him, nor for the endless chatter at the Academy... Especially, I wasn't interested in the "baby teeth" of pharmacology professor Yosi Zlokherson. My mind was elsewhere, in a "different place." It haunted my dreams and seemed as unattainable as peace was to the ancient Trojans. I dreamed, though distracted by the theft of my electrophoresis photos, notes, and protocols. (God forgive me, on which continent did these troubles begin?) I dreamed, even as viruses were uploaded to my laptop from a website praised by Olezhek. In Concordia, all my emails from the last two years in Kainman's lab were wiped out (after I had handed my laptop to a hospital worker at "Soroka" for repairs), leaving me powerless to prove the campaign against me, which had started back in America, or even earlier. I dreamed, distracted again by the direct sabotage of my experiments: contaminated cell cultures, mice disappearing right before experiments, the "accidental" repeated mixing of tubes by a treacherous collaborator in San Francisco. "Oops, I messed up again."

I involuntarily kept plasmids at home; when the fridge broke, they spoiled... Ultimately, Jacqueline threw my cells out of the liquid nitrogen container, and I was left with nothing to finish my paper, much less continue my San Francisco project. Around me buzzed tedious informers, tireless provocateurs, and complete psychos. They told me things, sometimes confidentially, sometimes angrily, but I didn't listen. "You need to help Jacqueline, pull out the good with the blood," whispered the omnipresent Olezhek.

"And don't tell anyone your reagents are missing," he added. "Don't."

Silver flashes flickered in the sky, and from all corners of the lab came deep voices chanting: "Give it back. Give it back. Just give it back." Yes, Olezhek was Kainman's mouthpiece... And Kainman, in turn, in his attempt to uncover my "great secrets," even called the police, and a small but efficient officer checked...

Did I call anyone on the "Sergio Kainman money" phone line from the office he himself gave me, supposedly so I could finish writing my article...? Suddenly, as if remembering, the officer reached for a box on the shelf filled with old articles and some useless stuff. Straining and bending awkwardly, the persistent policewoman managed to pull the box out but, after rummaging through its contents, pushed it aside with a sigh. Meanwhile, Kainman loomed in the doorway, watching her every move carefully. Sergio had pretended to meet me halfway, giving me a tiny room after he thought I'd suffered a "nervous breakdown."

The "office" was nothing more than a narrow, poorly plastered storage closet hastily cleared of garbage. A scratched-up table and a wobbly chair that creaked under me were crammed inside. In this so-called "office," they even managed to find a telephone socket and, as a "luxury," placed an old, cracked wired phone. Later, I found out I'd been cleverly set up...

Fortunately, I hadn't made a single call from that "office" phone. But was that the limit of Kainman's schemes? Horror and filth, blackmail and cynicism, rudeness and ignorance, how else could I describe the environment around me in Kainman's lab? And now, what awaits me? Will everything that happened once repeat again? With new actors and slightly changed scenery... But the real question, stark and clear, is: "Can I do science and..."

"To break oneself and become like Kainman, Zlokherson, and Roshti? Isn't it too late for that?" I wondered aloud. Perhaps the Lord showed mercy and opened my eyes... But why? Why did He do it after so many years?

"Are you serious?" Dimas nudged me and called out. "Does that happen to you often?"

"Not really... I was just lost in thought," I replied, pausing briefly.

"Come on, let's continue our conversation at the bar. I know a great place not far from here."

We walked down the well-lit street toward the bar. Once seated at the counter, Dimas began his monologue.

"Oh, those falling stars... Overblown superstitions. How many accidents have actually happened just because a black cat crossed someone's path? Does anyone even remember a single one? Look at these omens, they're like the 'voices' heard by the mentally ill. 'Do this. Don't do that.' Our world is full of paranoid schizophrenics, and that's a fact." Dimas settled comfortably into his favorite topic.

Honestly, how many people had bricks fall on them after crossing paths with a black cat while peacefully walking near their homes? How many slipped on an apple core, fell, and broke a leg just because they noticed the cheerfully wagging tail of a black cat? How many, distracted by the innocently purring black cat at a crosswalk, were struck by a speeding car, clearly exceeding the speed limit?

People believe in omens, pray, hope, and promise God they will become better, just to be spared from misfortune or to save their loved ones from incurable diseases... But all of this is empty.

"But they still say: 'There's some truth to it. Where there's smoke, there's fire,' and so on," I tried to argue.

"Yeah, right! Take, for example, a four-digit number where the sum of the first two digits equals the sum of the last two. A lucky number? 'Of course,' you'd say. But let's look at what happened during the so-called 'lucky' years of the 20th century..."

1919 – A tragic turning point in the Russian Civil War.

1928 – The beginning of large-scale repression in the USSR's industrial sector. Collectivization. 1937 – The bombing of Guernica; Stalin's repressions, historically known as 'the year 37.'

1946 – A symbolic beginning of the Cold War followed (in my opinion, justly) Churchill's speech in Fulton.

1955 – The Warsaw Pact was established. 1964 – Khrushchev was removed from power. The reforms ended.

1973 – The Yom Kippur War. Israel won, but many questions remained... 1982 – The rise to power of Andropov, a KGB official. 1991 – A reactionary coup attempt in Russia. Though suppressed, it was only temporary...

"And what about fortune-tellers? Don't they sometimes tell the truth?"

"There you go again. Your Kainman lies, shamelessly lies. He lies when he fabricates data. He lies when he accuses some poor soul of imaginable and unimaginable sins. And believe me, Kainman doesn't believe in omens... For him, integrity sounds like a pathology, and encyclopedic knowledge like a vice."

"Are you going to accuse Kainman of fabricating data again?"

"Yes."

"They'll kick you out of the hall again. And this time, they might even beat you up..."

"Don't worry. We know what we're doing..."

At that moment, a waitress approached and poured us some beer.

"So, where will you hunt him down now? They kicked you out of the lab..."

"Look at this," he said, pulling out his pass for the Keystone Conference.

We drank dark beer, eating burritos to go with it. Then we kept drinking... and drinking...

Late into the night, as we stepped out of the bar, he nodded at me and said goodbye: "Don't run straight. Not in circles, but diagonally..."

"What? What?" I asked again.

"Playing Russian roulette with Zlokherson, just like with Kainman, is no easy task... Well, goodbye." And he disappeared into a dark alley.

I felt Dimas wanted to say more, but I didn't press him. Suddenly, someone roughly bumped me with his shoulder and rushed out of the bar. It was a stranger who had been sitting across from us, scribbling nonstop without looking up. Without a word of apology, the stranger quickly followed Dimas into the alley...

A cold gust of wind brushed against my face. I raised my collar and headed home.

I feel like a Trojan.
Pressed against the shield on Troy's wall...
So many years I've spent—
(Persistence brings me no joy)—
Holding a circular defense above the steppe.

I feel like a Trojan.
Deaf to the clang of arms,
I blindly drag the horse into the city.
Pierced weakly by a spear,
(I cannot bear this mortal pain any longer...)

I feel like a Trojan.
Italy! Salvation is half the battle...
Oh gods, my end has yet to come.

And to begin life anew still isn't tiresome...
(Fools—hope—is it something I am not meant to know?)

II. At Home

I stepped out onto the balcony and looked at the "alien," wintry landscape from my apartment. A solitary streetlamp lit up a withered tree, stripped of all its leaves. From afar, it might have seemed like the ancient bones of a dinosaur lying at the bottom of a dried-up riverbed.

The short winter in Concordia is nothing like winter in Russia... Here, it's not just warmer; the trees themselves respond differently to the change in weather. Next to evergreen cypresses and olive trees stand yellowing oaks and bare maples... People, too, wrap themselves in warm jackets and coats, collars pulled up against the wind. It's hard to say, is this winter or merely a chilly autumn?

Hats of all styles, fedoras, cloches, berets, beanies, baseball caps, women's scarves, serve not only to keep our heads warm, but also to enhance our appearance, sometimes even signaling a person's degree of secularism or religious commitment.

Can I really add anything new about the role of religion in Concordia? So much has already been said and written... And yet, the spirit of Voltaire's age is still alive here. The problem is, there are no philosophers today with enough brilliance or courage to condemn the dominance of religion in the country's governmental institutions...

And the editors of the "police show" definitely picked up on my attitude toward religion... Everyone who had ever so much as "snitched" on me in America was portrayed as a devout, orthodox passerby. They would pause, glance in my direction as if catching every single thought I had about Kainman's lab in general, and about Olezhek in particular.

In my mind, I kept telling them to go to hell. Once, I couldn't hold back anymore and said to the actor sitting across from me, the one who would start fervently praying every time I thought about Olezhek: "What do you want?"

It's been five years since I returned to Concordia from the U.S. I still don't know which season I feel more at home in here, the dry, scorching summer or the cold, rainy winter. I don't know which is harder: being a "postdoc" in the American "show," or emitting thought energy in Concordia's labs (reading other people's thoughts is inappropriate, sure, but fascinating. Before you know it, you're hooked. And I don't know what's worse, being an assistant to Professor Sergio Kainman, or being his sworn enemy.

I keep waiting for a real job, one where they value you for the projects you propose. A job where you're hired not just to extract some "juicy bit," then tossed aside and smeared across the academic world as professionally incompetent. I keep waiting for the day when Kainman and his rivals in the scientific community will want to publish my project... But it's all in vain.

Sometimes, I feel like any moment now, someone will finally say: "Enough! How much longer can we keep tormenting this poor mother and her son?" But again, nothing...

I walked back into the room. The TV was showing a football match. The German national team was playing, but I do not remember against whom. I think I finally understand what "total football" really means.

At the supermarket, someone stole my shopping cart while I was turned around paying at the register. The customers in line and the cashier all chuckled...

At the Ministry of Absorption (Immigration), they handed me a booklet of benefits, only after those benefits had already expired. And when I later called the same ministry to request a job (or at least a job interview), as is customary for new immigrants, laughter echoed through the phone: "What job? Your work is already done. Besides, we've offered you interviews six or seven times already, and you refused." Then came a long beep, the call was disconnected.

Suddenly, the television "broke" Cable broadcasting stopped completely. In its place appeared twelve strange channels. On one, a "festive" military parade in North Korea. On another, a feature film about the crucifixion of Jesus Christ. There were also tabloid news stories, like the one about a billionaire woman who got pregnant by an ageless gigolo who also robbed her.

Each of these programs would restart the moment they ended. The military parade, in particular, seemed to last an eternity...

And the crowning jewel of this television programming, the cherry on top of the media madness, turned out to be James Bond, staring directly into the screen and repeatedly saying: "If you want to take revenge on someone, first make sure you've dug your own grave."

Suddenly, the window burst open with a loud noise, and a strong gust of wind swept the papers off my desk and spilled my coffee. I closed the window, wiped down the table, and after gathering everything from the floor, I walked over to the bookshelf.

That's where I'd placed my lab notebooks from America... Or at least, that's where I had put them when I returned to Concordia. But now, they were gone.

They had vanished.

At work, Dusty was raging: "Do you understand Concordian? Or what language do I need to speak with you? Do your dreams bother you?"

The dreams had started "bothering" me back in the Soviet Union... Once, I dreamt that someone, just like many years later in America and Concordia, was interrogating me, persistently asking: "Who would you choose to survive, your mother or your father?"

And two days before my father's death, I had a dream that he was dying. I woke up, and an unfamiliar inner voice whispered to me: "Spit over your left shoulder, and your father will live."

"Screw that," I thought. "I don't believe in such silly superstitions."

And I didn't spit...My father died two days later. The "emergency" ambulance, summoned on an urgent call, took an unreasonably long time to arrive. By the time the doctors got there, it was too late, there was nothing they could do.

Now, I spit over my left shoulder for every reason and no reason at all. I'm terrified. Not so much for myself, but for my mother.

"By the way, does your leg still bother you?" Dusty interrupted my thoughts.

I was struck in the left leg during a run in Denver, just before I left for San Francisco. Three or four doctors I visited openly mocked me, showing me pictures of ligaments from anatomy textbooks or telling me to increase physical activity to "strengthen the muscles." They smirked at something I couldn't understand...

The waiting room at the clinic was full of inmates in orange jumpsuits, handcuffed and shackled, guarded by bored police officers jingling their keys. Apparently, no other patients were being admitted during those days.

Eventually, an elderly Jewish doctor fitted my leg with a brace. I wore it for six months.

Before that, my foot was a swirl of every sea and sky color from Aivazovsky's paintings, and even unlaced sneakers were a struggle to get on. That was their way of punishing me, for leaving.

In San Francisco, I took another hit to the leg, during a soccer match, from a lab tech from Denver, whom I'd met through Hans (also formerly from Denver).
He missed by just a few centimeters, nearly striking my ankle joint. Oddly, the ball was nowhere near me...

"It's fine, it's fine," Olezhek smirked. "In other countries, people are dying of hunger..." Apparently, he had been standing among the spectators, generously handing out his "valuable" commentary.

Limping slightly, I returned to the lab. My "well-wishers" were probably hoping I'd be forced to hand off the project due to an injury-related absence, if my ankle had been damaged. This time, they miscalculated.

I started coughing and nearly collapsed. Dusty, whether out of sympathy or politeness, remarked, "You really should see a doctor."

"I already saw a pulmonologist. He told me I'm coughing because I'm fat." (Even though I weighed the same a month ago and wasn't coughing then.)

"And what did he recommend?"

"To drink warm water…"

My mobile phone started vibrating and ringing. It was my primary care doctor calling.

"I have your test results. There's good news and bad news…"

"Let's start with the bad."

"You have whooping cough."

"That's odd. I had it as a child…"

"Well, you'll need to stay home, at least to avoid passing out at work, like you nearly did in my office. Take some time to rest. Oh, and by the way, where on earth did you catch whooping cough?"

"I don't know. One of the lab assistants was coughing all day at work…"

William Roshti stepped out of his office, exclaiming enthusiastically: "What a mafioso Shmulik is! Getting such a huge grant, incredible!"

I tried to interrupt and start a conversation.

"I spoke with Sergio Kainman... I'm ready to be of use and to discuss which part of my project I could pass on to you..."

Roshti's expression changed. "I'll find you in the lab," he said curtly, looking straight through me.

Passing by, Yossi Zlokherson smirked...

Apparently, it's time for me to "prepare a parachute" (in plain language, start looking for a job). Disheartened, I walked into my room and found the enormous lab assistant Tatyana (nicknamed "the encyclopedia of other people's lives") rifling through a folder of my lab notes and documents lying on the desk.

Not finding what she was looking for, Tatyana opened my personal laptop.

"Need some help?" I asked.

Tatyana coughed and, without missing a beat, asked, as if reciting a memorized poem: "Did you return the basket with ice to its place?"

"As far as I know, yes."

"Well, I'm sure, no."

The next morning, when I arrived at work, I saw Tatyana moving the basket to a different table. Now I understood why...

Two Chinese lab assistants burst into the room. They started shouting over each other, mangling my name:
"Volodiiia, you didn't return the electrophoresis slides to their place!"

Without letting me speak, they kept going: "This is not good, Volodiiia, you must return things to where they belong. This is very not good. Return our slides immediately, you hear? We've been looking for them all day."

One of them, the older one, stopped in front of me, looked me straight in the eye, and said confidently, in perfect Russian: "Leave. Nobody here likes you. Why won't you leave?"

Tatyana let out a snide laugh.

"I just wanted to say... the slides have been in the cabinet in your room for quite a while," I tried to object.

"What are you telling him for? He argues with everyone... By the way, he also broke our homogenizer!" Tatyana chimed in.

"Alright!" The Chinese assistants suddenly calmed down and fled like gazelles, shouting something between themselves, just as abruptly as they had arrived.

"I didn't even touch your homogenizer," I tried to defend myself.

Dusty appeared in the doorway. She winked cheerfully at Tatyana, mimicked someone, then disappeared.

"Volodya, do you want to meet three beauties?" Tatyana asked me once Dusty's door had closed. She stared at her computer without looking up.

"Somewhere I've heard about the three beauties before," I thought, but aloud I only said: "What beauties are you talking about?"

"The ones who came from your former lab... Olezhek, Antoshka, and Zhenyechka, remember them? Missing the warm days, huh?"

In my room, gleaming with paint and varnish,
A school globe sits like a stranger's child.
It stands, skewed upon a tilted axis,
And flies through space and time and through
Unbounded vastness, impenetrable darkness.
Why I gaze upon it, I do not understand.

A school globe, a simple, unassuming thing.
Why then does it seem so lonely and ominous?
To understand this, I flung wide open
My windows, like six seraphic wings.

—Pavel Antokolsky

III. The Visit of the Little Black Man

"You're here again?"

"Where would you go without me?"

"Why did you transport me to the future?"

"So that you would understand..."

"Understand what?"

"That it's necessary to stop harboring illusions... and being fixated on your inner world..."

"Why didn't you transport me to the past then?"

"You know, that can be fixed..."

"No, wait."

"Too late..."

The room spun around me... I closed my eyes and leaned my head back against the chair. I woke up in a laboratory. Around me stood jars and test tubes filled with solutions and powders. I heard a muffled, quiet conversation involving two people. I recognized Zlokherson's low voice and Glenke's voice, tinkling like a falling spoon.

"So you'll do as we agreed," Zlokherson said.

"Yes!" Glenke replied abruptly and confidently.

"Give him the exam questions and leave him alone in your office. It'll be enough for him to just flip through them and change the order... The university police will notice this and report it to the dean of the pharmacology school... We'll accuse Volodya of distributing exam questions among students... And then no one will reproach us for putting a crazy person into a correctional show..."

Both entered the laboratory from the office... and the room, and the objects in it, flickered, spinning again above my head...

And now I see myself in Glenke's office. On the desk lies a folder with exam questions... I am working on a laptop... For a moment, I break away and fix my gaze on the folder... Mechanically, I reach out and... And then I shout to myself: "Wait! Don't touch the exam questions!"

But I don't hear myself and take two sheets from the stack, glance through them, and carelessly place them on top of the pile...

The room blurs and disappears, and I find myself in the dean's office. The dean sits at his desk, head bowed, wincing as he reads some letter. Glenke, digging her long nails into the armrests of the chair, is literally fixated on the dean with her eyes... Zlokherson is by the window, pretending not to follow what's happening, looking at something outside...

"Well then, what have you decided to do?" Glenke breaks the silence.

"Understand," the dean replies, looking up from the letter and folding his glasses. "To put a person in such a show for life—that is very cruel. Especially since you have next to no proof... Zlokherson's student, Leila, saw two young people cooing at Lisitsky's birthday. Lisitsky himself is a dark and untrustworthy character. How he got his diploma is a big question... This is already a trend; first, there was Alexander Tsimerman, whom you slipped into Volodya's dormitory... It's also unclear how he finished his studies and became a pharmacist..." And the dean looked at Zlokherson questioningly... Zlokherson, without taking his gaze from the window, ignored the dean's barb...

"And finally, the main thing: the two sheets moved from the folder with the questions are by no means proof of Volodya's guilt..."

"So, are you suggesting we take him to court and imprison him, and then strip him of his third degree?" Zlokherson interrupted imperiously. "You also tried to catch Volodya with girls... We supported you in the elections... Next time, we can vote for your opponent."

"Alright," the dean said after a long pause, holding his head with both hands. "I will contact Soroka Hospital and the special services... In Sweden, I suppose everything is ready for his visit..."

"Yes, they're expecting him in 3 months," Glenke quickly replied.

"But do you understand that something we wouldn't want to hear might surface?"

"We understand," Glenke responded, "but there's no choice..."

And the room, along with the people in it, folded like a house of cards. I was sitting in front of the computer again. The little man in the black frock coat was broadcasting from the screen.

"Well?" he asked. "Did you go into the past? Has it sunk in now?"

"I can't change anything anymore... And I doubt I could have, even if I lived my life over again..."

One goes by the straight path,

Another goes in circles

And waits for return to the ancestral home,

Waits for the former girlfriend.

But I go—behind me is trouble,

Neither straight nor crooked,

But into nowhere and into never,

Like trains off a cliff.

—*Anna Akhmatova*

IV. The Rolling Stone

From the moment I stepped into the office, I could tell William Roshti was in a foul mood... He was smoking, biting his cigarette, deleting and retyping text on his computer, muttering curses in both English and Concordian. Without looking at me, Roshti nodded. Then, spinning his chair around, he moved closer to his desk.

"I need to know if you want to stay in my lab."

"Yes, of course I do," I replied, feigning confusion.

"Then tell me, what were you working on in San Francisco?"

"Mitochondria..."

"Volodya, a man with your past won't get hired anywhere else... But I took you in. Besides, no one will pass you by the next time you look for a job. They'll ask me to give you a recommendation... I hope you understand now how unenviable your position is."

"I was studying the role of mitochondria in senescence..."

I tried to steer the conversation in another direction, just as Kainman had once taught me when we were still on good terms. "I'm writing a review article. I can include your name. I can even increase your salary..."

Roshti's anger shifted to mercy.

"That works for me. I was studying the role of the mitochondrial transporter in glucose-induced senescence... The nuance was that during senescence, cells stop dividing and start producing inflammatory proteins... Meanwhile, cells lacking the transporter do indeed stop dividing, but the synthesis of certain inflammatory proteins is disrupted... So most likely, this transporter isn't involved in senescence..."

"Alright," Roshti said weakly, turning back to his computer.

I left the room, having earned a spot in the review article and some peace at work, for a while.

I took back the flash drive with the file I'd saved for Roshti. It contained my proposals.

As I exited the building, I threw the flash drive at the nearest car. Pushing it to make sure the alarm sounded, I stepped aside and then looked back.

Near the parking lot, a commotion was underway...

A security guard was nearby. The car belonged to one of the professors...

The guard noticed the flash drive. He picked it up from the asphalt, turned it over and over in his hands, then slipped it into his trouser pocket.

I see a stony sky
Above the dim web of waters.

In the grip of loathsome Erebus,
The soul agonizingly lives.

I understand this horror
And grasp this connection:
The sky falls without shattering,
The sea splashes without foaming.

Oh, pale wings of the chimera,
On coarse gold of the sand,
And sails like gray trefoils,
Crucified like my sorrow!

—Osip Mandelstam

V. Akmol

The coniferous forest ended, giving way to what could have been either steppe or a strange desert dotted with sparse shrubs. From the window of the bus winding along a narrow, twisting road, it was impossible to tell exactly what lay beyond.

Meanwhile, the suburbs of the city of Akmol appeared on the horizon like ancient, earthen burial mounds of vanished chieftains. The relentless sun spared no one who failed to find refuge in the shade of broad-leaved, solitary trees or beneath the awning of some tall building.

The people of Concordia here resembled the inhabitants of Zelotania: both wore mustaches and bore the marks of sunburn. As a well-known Russian-speaking writer and artist in Concordia once said about the residents of Akmol, "They all had the same goal in their eyes."

As that same writer once admitted, "Akmol was a city I did not love for personal reasons."

Akmol, I say... When I emigrated from Russia to Concordia, Akmol was the first city to greet me with its "fiery" embrace. Here, I experienced hunger and poverty. Here, I underwent two rather unsuccessful surgeries, one after the other. The surgeons, shaking my hand firmly, blamed each other with special thoroughness for their professional failures.

Here, I encountered, unfortunately, not for the first or last time, the depths of human stupidity and primitiveness.

After moving in search of work from Akmol to a nearby agricultural settlement, I asked a local man named Itzik to make frames for paintings I had brought from Russia. Itzik examined them carefully, and his gaze lingered on one painting depicting a tombstone with a cross. Turning the painting this way and that, he asked me, "Volodya, are you really Jewish?"

And soon across the Concordian steppe, the cry went up: "Volodya is not Jewish..."

But shaking off those unpleasant memories, I jumped briskly off the bus steps at the first stop in Akmol and waited until the bus passed.

On the count of three, the traffic light turned green, and I ran across the road, entering the university campus, whose central library resembled a Chinese...

The university library resembled a pagoda. I walked around it and, in high spirits, quickened my pace toward the building housing Professor Angelina Shushants' laboratory... She was my "parachute."

Angelina Shushants specialized in mitochondria and, in particular, one of the mitochondrial transporters. I had worked on that same transporter in Sergio Kainman's lab... As an "academic hobby," she also tried her hand at gathering information about Latin Americans from the institutions where I had previously worked.

In the first days of my work in her lab, Professor Shushants praised me repeatedly, but gradually she slid into confrontation with me... As had happened before, at past workplaces, the entire lab, or at least most of it—participated in the wild, dirty chaos controlled from above.

"Angelina Pustovoitova," hissed from every corner of the serpentarium...

"Friend and wife, but not yours," crackled everywhere like a broken radio.

In the end, I found myself in Angelina Shushants' spacious, brand-new office with large windows through which warm, untouched sunlight poured in. Angelina Shushants puzzled me...

I was faced with a dilemma: either I gave her the project, or I walked out of her lab on the spot.

Let me know if you'd like to emphasize tension, resentment, or formality.

Several years before this conversation, during my last visit to Concordia from San Francisco, I met with Ilya Besslovesny, with whom I had once studied for my third academic degree. But back then, Ilya's main job was to sniff out, spy, and report… Despite never having published a single article during his postdoc, he secured a laboratory at Akmol University.

He suggested I meet with Angelina Shushants to "discuss" the project I was working on with Sergio Kainman, specifically the mitochondrial transporter…

Amid the wail of a piercing ambulance siren and a fine drizzle, we entered a bar. Throughout our rather long conversation, I didn't utter a single word about my work, yet Ilya demonstrated "impressive" knowledge about both my project and the dynamics among the students in Kainman's lab.

I had never imagined he could be so talkative… Ilya even knew that my fellowship had not been renewed, though I had never breathed a word about it or my project to anyone in Concordia.

All of this was politely conveyed to me during a confidential conversation over a mug of beer…

The staunch teetotaler Ilya Besslovesny, who had never touched alcohol anywhere or at any time, went with me to the bar for the sake of…

…to convince me to "sell" the project to Angelina Shushants and, in return, apparently secure a lab at Akmol University for himself. He "humbly" hoped to receive a spin-off of my project as a fee for his mediation.

I disliked this proposal, as well as his "intimate knowledge" of my work in San Francisco, and I refused to meet with Angelina Shushants or negotiate behind Sergio Kainman's back.

Alas, the value of my project diminished over the years I spent in Concordia, and my situation became increasingly hopeless...

> *But I won't bore the reader with a detailed account of my brief further stay in Angelina Shushants' lab.*
>
> *In short, I parted ways with her too... Sveridov was right, there is no romance where an impenetrable, viscous, rotten swamp swirls.*
>
> *You led so recklessly through the rough terrain,*
> *Like a falling star in the dark abyss. You were bitterness and deceit, And comfort—never.*
>
> *—Anna Akhmatova*

VI. Antoshka and Katya.

"Only losers date Black people," Antoshka suddenly blurted out for no clear reason and slammed the pipette down on the table. It clattered loudly, and the red ribbon with the hammer and sickle emblazoned on it, which framed the pipette, spread out flat across the desk. Antoshka first pressed it down with his thumb, then, realizing what he'd done, tried unsuccessfully to peel it off the table with a pocket knife.

He knew my ex-girlfriend was African American, but that didn't stop him...

"Well, now it's Black people. Before it was Russian Jews, Jewish banks in America that wouldn't lend to 'honest' citizens, the Holocaust, and the cult of a personality 'that never was...' What or who's next?" I thought to myself.

Sergio Kainman was an experienced manipulator. And if he needed to push a weak spot, mine was clearly the Jewish...

If the topic was sensitive, he wouldn't hesitate to push it, even though he himself was Jewish... Kainman skillfully pitted students against each other, shielding himself from any intrigue.

"Antoshka, where are you?" called his wife, Katya. She worked as Kainman's secretary. "The chicken's ready."

"Did you hear? The Ukrainians have elected a new president..."

"If I were the president of Russia, I'd send tanks into Kyiv," Antoshka hissed.

"Antoshka, are you drunk again?"

Antoshka opened his already wide eyes even wider, which now gleamed with an unhealthy shine. He stared at the floor but said nothing... Antoshka often got drunk to the point of blackout and skipped work.

"I'm so fed up with this Kainman," Katya continued, "If I were his wife, I'd definitely put him in his place..."

"Katya! Everything depends on Kainman..." Antoshka finally responded.

"Antoshka, I can't," Katya said, bursting into tears.

"Maybe I'll go," I said uncertainly.

"You read such interesting articles," Antoshka said to me. "What? What is it?"

"Just know this—if you want to stage a revolution in the lab, you have to do it from behind the scenes," Antoshka called after me.

I had no intention of starting a revolution in the lab. That was for sure! Antoshka had a knack for making his listener feel like a part of his story...

It turned out Antoshka learned about the "interesting articles" I was reading from the department's IT guy, to whom I had handed my not-so-old laptop for repairs. He had copied all the files from my computer, including links to the articles, and passed them on to Antoshka. At the same time, he rudely refused to fix my laptop, advising me to just buy a new one...

A couple of days later, Kainman caught me in the corridor and sneered:

"Volodya, you're reading some 'interesting articles.'"

"I already know," I snapped, realizing I'd been marked with a black pirate's brand... "Happy holiday to you." This conversation took place on Rosh Hashanah, the Jewish New Year.

"And have you been to the synagogue to pray yet?"

"No, I play in a different league..."

"And you don't play Sport Lotto?" he asked, laughing and baring his wolfish grin. After laughing heartily, Kainman spun around a full 180 degrees, and the gleam of his pristine white nape shone down the corridor.

That wasn't the only incident between Antoshka and me. One evening, when I entered the lab, I overheard Olezhek say, "We need to get Volodya's proposal as soon as possible. Have you talked to Rain yet?" Rain worked in the pharmacology department's HR office and handled grants and scientific proposals. Once he hinted to me, "I could even be your friend. Bring me some booze." Apparently, Antoshka delivered...

Antoshka was not only a thief, informant, and provocateur but also a saboteur. He gave me a DNA vector that didn't work. In moments of spite, he would toss out other people's mice when passing by their cages or sneak some nastiness into the cells, and so on. In war, all means are good, and Antoshka used lies from the Denver mafia and Zlokherson from Concordia to turn both Kainman and Jacqueline against me and to wrest my project away.

Once, during a heated lab argument, Antoshka showed me a syringe with an uncovered needle, "You know what this is, Volodya?" Hans chuckled approvingly in the corridor... The matter was swept under the rug. The very next day, Antoshka was smiling at me as if nothing had happened...

Antoshka provided me with an incomplete protocol and got two in return. Moreover, I suggested measuring mitochondrial mass in his cells. I conducted an experiment for Antoshka that demonstrated my theory worked. I committed to several more experiments for him, which made up the first article and formed the basis of his second article with a South Korean postdoc. Yet neither Antoshka nor Kainman credited me in their papers... And my email to Antoshka with my scientific proposals mysteriously disappeared—not only from my computer but also from the university server, as if it never existed...

When Olezhek "convinced" my acquaintance Shuli to record our conversation on her phone, and then triumphantly said, "Bye, Volodya," Antoshka got up from the table, made a mocking face, and stared at me, coughing with a whistle...

Antoshka was cheerfully exchanging glances with John as John, following Jacqueline's orders, unplugged (about five or six times) the power supply connected to my electrophoresis equipment in the cold room. Antoshka found it funny.

"You're a crazy paranoid," his friend Sasha, the computer guy, once remarked to him. It was Sasha who helped Katya write strange messages, supposedly from my friends, to my email or to my Odnoklassniki profile. Katya, or rather my "friends" from all over the world, advised me to visit a porn site, find myself a Ukrainian girl, or go to Ukraine to search for earrings from ancient people...

I kept silent about the first two suggestions. But I responded to the invitation for archaeological digs: "So, you don't have any problem with earrings then."

Antoshka had given Katya earrings for one of her birthdays, and I reminded Katya about them... After that, all messages from my "friends" stopped. However, phone calls began, with long, continuous silence on the line, or a "warrior-like," childish cry: "We are coming."

"Volodya, I called you," Katya screamed, fixing her hair.

"Uh... I guess I wasn't home," I inserted the first reply that came to mind into the "fragile" remains of our brief conversation. I left the room where I was working with cell cultures, so the conversation wouldn't drag on.

And in the warm and decisive August, shortly before my return from San Francisco to Concordia, the computer guy, Sasha, approached me twice in the university cafeteria with a proposal to hand over my project to Antoshka. He told me it would be a good idea to bring my mother from Concordia to the USA, that I had already spent a lot of money on a lawyer to get an American Green Card, that it was hard to find a job in Concordia... and so on and so forth. I refused twice.

It doesn't matter that you've been hit by chance,
It doesn't matter that you're not a fighter by stance.
What matters is that in this world still remain
Duels that hold its fragile frame.

It doesn't matter if you survive the strife,
It doesn't matter if your anger fades from life.
What matters is that in this world still exist
Grudges that cannot be dismissed.

It doesn't matter if foolish postures confuse,
It doesn't matter if you lack the gunman's use.
What matters is that in this world there are fights,
And some questions can only be solved by such rites.

—Leonid Filatov

VII. Sergio Kainman

"All right," I said to myself. "Let me try to come to an agreement with Kainman." Since Jacqueline had officially announced at the lab meeting: *"Bring Sergio a big story and you'll stay in the lab for another year,"* I decided to take them at their word.

I went to Kainman and brought him three projects (not including my main one). He turned over in his hands a new diagram I had drawn showing the involvement of mitochondria in the inflammatory process, smiled, and said, "Good, go ahead and work on these projects, but don't forget your main one." He kept the sheet with the diagram.

A few weeks later, at a party at Kainman's place, Olezhek said to me, "Come, let's listen to what Sergio has to say. He loves dogs so much." We walked over to Kainman. Olezhek pointed out a dog playing on the lawn: "Sergio, is this breed of dog smart?"

"The breed is smart, but this dog is stupid," Kainman laughed.

He looked at me. He couldn't *not* know that the word "Dog" in Concordia was used for the worst kind of outcasts...

But that wasn't enough for Kainman, he even sent Zhenya after me in the lab. Zhenya, an avid motorcyclist and a blabbermouth, whispered to me with an unnatural gleam in his eye, "Strictly off the record: Sergio doesn't like it when students come begging right after getting invited."

I didn't say anything, just buried my face in a test tube.

Then he added, "Too bad you didn't come to Antoshka's on Sunday... There were some *really* hot girls there."

Strangely, I started getting "randomly" approached on my way to work by other members of Kainman's group. One after another, they kept trying to convince me to "go talk to Sergio." Apparently, he was "tough, but fair"...

"You really need to talk to him, ASAP," said some old hag who plopped down next to me at the bar. "Well, if you won't go see *him*," she added, "then come home with *me*... I'm not letting you off that easy."

"Thanks for the invite," I replied dryly. I got up, paid my bill, and walked away from the bar counter.

I knew myself that I needed to clear the air with Kainman. So I tried to meet with him again. But it was useless.

He was always busy with something and couldn't talk to me... Whether it was him or his secretary, the answer to my requests was always the same: no.

Then my salary wasn't paid for a whole month. After that, my scholarship expired, and oddly, it was extended for only four months instead of the full year...

Eventually, I managed to catch Kainman outside his office and asked him, "So... should I just leave?"

"Wait," he said offhandedly, then shut the door in my face and disappeared into his office.

Even then, my fate was being decided, quietly, but inevitably: If Kainman managed to sell my projects, I'd be forced to leave the lab. If he *didn't* sell them, maybe I'd be allowed to stick around a little longer... the whole *schtick* (Yiddish for "flavor" or "trick") was in bringing a student's project to a point where its direction and continuation became obvious, and once that happened, you could do whatever you wanted with the project... and with the student.

And to top it all off, Sergio Kainman was a coward. A *Member of the American Academy of Science*, former science advisor to the U.S. government, current professor at the University of California, San Francisco, and yet, he was afraid to publish anything that might provoke a mixed reaction from his colleagues.

Before submitting a paper to a scientific journal, he would first "leak" the manuscript to a few trusted scientists, whose opinions he trusted. And if the project didn't get the "green light," Kainman preferred to *sell* it off to other, already "high-ranking" figures in the scientific world.

The problem wasn't with the projects, it was with the people he trusted. On top of that, Kainman didn't want to "get involved" with the powerful *patrons* backing certain students working in his lab. He was also terrified (*panicked*, really) at the thought of loud, explosive "scandals" erupting in the HR Department, which traditionally protected postdocs from Third World countries.

Shortly after one of the parties at Kainman's house (Antoshka used to call it "the lair"), one of Sergio's students, Doli came up to me and informed me that, most likely, my transporter wasn't involved in regulating the protein complex responsible for the inflammatory response.

Which meant the whole theory was wrong... Which meant I had handed Kainman *garbage*.

All the while, she didn't show me a single real image.

She didn't show me any actual electrophoresis images, claiming they were "of poor quality."

I didn't know what else to do, so I wrote her an email:

"Thanks a lot. However, I don't share your thinking, and I didn't ask you to perform this experiment. Hence,

I don't need your help anymore. Thank you for your cooperation."

She replied:

"I am a Christian. I cannot lie."

To which I responded:

"I consider your words very insulting. I wish you only the best."

Later, when Sergio Kainman happened to be walking down the corridor, I stepped out to meet him. I wanted to look him in the eye. But instead, I once again saw that familiar wolfish grin, his strong front teeth bared as always. We didn't greet each other.

Shortly after, Kainman submitted a written explanation to HR, in which among other things, he claimed that *I* didn't want to share with him...

Of course, Kainman

Naturally, Kainman didn't mention how he had once told me, "Don't get attached to data," twisting a quote from some dumb movie, as he slashed down my main project.

Kainman needed extra projects. He had around thirty postdocs, and not enough ideas to go around... And I was "difficult," hardened by bitter experience. I didn't have enough projects for all of Kainman's students. And handing over the future of my main project, that was a red line I wasn't willing to cross.

That would've meant the end of my academic career.

Once, in San Francisco, I got a call from Hélène Grenke. I hadn't spoken to her since our PhD days. Grenke offered me a two-year position in her lab, funded by the Concordian pharmaceutical company *Forest*.

I politely declined.

A couple of years later, during our last meeting, Kainman suddenly said to me:

"Without my permission, *Forest* won't run a single experiment."

"Jacqueline! 'The cavalry won't get through here,'" it seemed to me that Sergio Kainman was quoting Walter Scott. "Deal with Volodya yourself!" he shouted at her...

And Jacqueline dealt with it. They left me working in the lab without a salary and without a budget for reagents.
Almost every day there were some kinds of conflicts with other postdocs or lab technicians. There were outright acts of sabotage and failures to fulfill prior commitments by scientists from other labs, Kainman's students, or even biotech companies...

After some time had passed, the project that Doli had said proved the whole theory false was published in *Nature* by Professor Frank Chopp from Switzerland. Professor Chopp was the scientific editor of this journal and a few other "top-tier" scientific publications... Unlike me, Kainman knew how to "sell" ideas, even if they weren't his own.

A few months later, Sergio summoned me to his office.
He immediately got straight to the point, without even looking at my recent

He didn't even glance at my recent results before saying,
"I need your project. In return, you'll get a job at a biotech company in America."

"And six months from now, I'll be out of work, without a publication, and with a ruined CV?" I asked.

"Well, suit yourself," he replied casually, rising from behind the wide desk cluttered with papers, articles, a laptop, and a photo of his wife and kids.

The brief audience was over... and I had just signed my own inevitable death sentence.

Now, Kainman's carefully crafted, damning dossier, the "Zlokherson file" would follow me around the world.
And in the television "quiz show" called *The Same*, Kainman and Zlokherson would walk away "unscathed" or "off the hook."

Kainman, in fact, "spent his entire conscious life playing with toy soldiers, only when he grew up did the soldiers become real people," as the classic writer put it.

Night. Street. Lamp. Drugstore.

A dull and meaningless glow.

Live on a quarter-century more—

It will be just so. There's no way to go.

You'll die—and start it all again,

The same as in years before:

Night. The icy ripple of a drain.

The drugstore. The street. The lamp. Once more.

—Aleksandr Block

VIII. The Last Battle of Arabella

In the Concordian night sky, there were very few stars (not like in Crimea!). And a bright white star, detached from the crescent moon, shone alone... It was the flickering light of a solitary airship. The airship hovered above the city center, carelessly swaying in gusts of strong wind.

In our lives, everyone is watching someone, like stern judges at a competition... It's a shame that in real life, we're not just playing for trophies, but for a place in the sun. Not for fun, but very seriously... And our loved ones, friends, and colleagues, they're with us only as long as we score goals against others. And if we don't score, others will, and very likely, those goals will be scored against us...

"Volodya, where are you? How long must I search for you?" shouted Professor William Roshti, kicking a basket of ice that held my test tubes. Some of the tubes fell out. Luckily, they were tightly sealed.

"I was working in the cold room," I called back, picking up the tubes.

"You left the lab without turning off the lights."

"I was just about to go back."

"You didn't unplug the power supply," Roshti said sharply.

"I'm going to work with it."

"I sent you emails from India. Why didn't you reply to any of them?"

"I didn't receive any messages from you."

"So am I lying?"

I stayed silent.

"What's wrong with the cells? Why are they contaminated?" Roshti pressed on. "You already know... I wish I knew myself why."

"What? What does that mean?" Roshti continued, clearly irritated.

"Have you read the abstract with my proposals?" I tried to change the subject, hoping to ease the tension. "Yes. It doesn't suit me. It's not my area."

"But it could be a new function of the transporter you're studying..."

"So what? It doesn't fit, and that's that."

He twitched, sucking in his cheeks. "Fine. Work for one more month. But not on the abstract," Roshti tossed at me on his way out, slamming the door loudly behind him.

No wonder he hadn't published a single article in over ten years. How he hadn't been fired from the university was a mystery. And, on top of that, he was allowed to sit on the committee handing out grants for conference travel. They say the late Father William

Roshti was a luminary in science, with powerful connections...

No sooner had the door closed behind him than the gloomy lab tech, Tatiana, fierce as a wild beast, stormed out into the hall and attacked me. "What's wrong with the cells I gave you?"

"What cells? Some are contaminated, others won't proliferate, even though they're on different shelves in the incubator..."

"You don't know how to work with cells..."

"Doubt it," I muttered. "And you have communication problems with people, too," Tatiana almost shouted, slamming the door behind her in anger, just like Roshti.

From the storage closet poked out the disheveled, wild-haired head of the student Dusty. "I heard your conversation. What cells are you talking about? Immune cells derived from breast cancer tumor cells?"

"What breast cancer? Are you even listening to yourself?"

"Is it true that Iyal (the only reliable lab worker) has a chair with a tall back?"

"Don't worry about him getting fired," Dusty blurted out like a programmed robot.

"That's a real shame! Iyal's a good guy," I replied.

Dusty wet her hands and shook them sharply, even nervously, a few times over the sink. Without drying them, she turned to me. "So, is this your office?" she nodded toward the cold room.

"No, not really. Just making do…"

"Uh-huh. Making do…"

"What do you think?" Dusty pressed on, relentless. "Will William Roshti take me back to his lab after a year away? I'm planning to work a bit in a biotech company…"

And with that, she ducked back into the storage closet without waiting for my answer.

Oh, these dear "admirers" of mine… Clearly, they never flipped through

One Day in the Life of Ivan Denisovich.

They had other life textbooks.

Everything I wrote back then
inevitably ended in ellipses.
I fell, unbuttoned,
onto my bed. And if at night
I found a star upon the ceiling,
it, by the laws of burning out,
would run down my cheek to the pillow
faster than I could make a wish.

—Joseph Brodsky

IX. In The Stone Halls

I stopped at the entrance of a shabby, gloomy, stone two-story building with a half-collapsed balcony. My attention was caught by a simple, solitary daisy pushing its way through the stones, adorning the entrance to this "ruin of the Parthenon."

This was where my next psychologist had arranged to meet me.

I arrived ahead of time, and there was no harm in spending a few minutes admiring this little wonder, the city daisy.

Its white petals seemed to reach out to me, as if saying, "Don't worry. Everything will be all right."

But it was time to go... The psychologist had asked me not to be late for the appointment, as her schedule was packed.

I pushed open the door and stepped inside the building.

What I saw was the complete opposite of the building's exterior.

The shiny, brand-new tiled floors and walls absorbed and reflected the light from numerous lamps. Green plants in brown pots, meticulously cleaned on the outside, seemed to fill the lobby with oxygen and beauty...

Despite being only two stories, the building had an elevator, which I took to the second floor.

The psychologist turned out to be a middle-aged, slender woman with dyed hair, heavily powdered, dressed in a gray "office" suit consisting of a jacket and skirt.
Adding to the picture, she wore the jacket over a fresh, neatly ironed white blouse... Her name was Iren Marnavsky.

"Please, Volodya," Iren smiled, gesturing to the chair.

"Good afternoon, Iren," I replied, settling comfortably into the deep armchair.

"What shall we talk about today?" Iren asked, smoothing her skirt and putting on a serious expression.

"Anything, even eggplants," I laughed.

"We'll leave eggplants for better times... How's your health? Any improvement since we started our sessions?"

"Thanks, I felt better when I was eighteen..."

"I'm not asking what you felt at eighteen. After all, you've always felt bad or very bad..."

(I wondered how she knew that.)

"Alright, let's change the subject. Are you working anywhere? Are you still thinking about your project?"

"My answer to the first question is 'No.' To the second, 'Yes.'"

"Volodya, you've got one convoluted brain fold, but it's a fold above all folds! You're a hen laying golden eggs, why not go into neuroscience or switch to or change your profession? You need to measure your strength and talents... Say 'goodbye' to the past... Change the rules of the game."

"I can't, got to protect the eggs," I said. "But seriously, the past is our life. Maybe lived, but still life. You understand? The past shapes who we are now. And sometimes there's nothing harder than continuing our past in the present... Putting all the dots over the i's... Understanding and accepting mistakes, and finishing the work of a lifetime..."

"You have to learn from the past, but you can't live in it," Iren replied.

How old are you? Forty-two? Forty-three?"

"Forty-five."

"You're only just beginning to live."

A long, awkward silence fell between us, uncomfortable, but brief.

"Listen," Iren broke the quiet, "have you tried writing down everything that's happened to you? To, you know, let off some steam..."

"Write down *everything*?"

"Well, at least part of it... What troubles you most..."

"But the book will just end up in a drawer anyway."

"So, what... at least you'll get to speak your mind... and stop dwelling on your past."

"I'll think about it," I said hesitantly, pulling my bag closer.

"Think it over. But for now, it's my session again... Set your bag aside. Nobody will steal it in my office. Make yourself comfortable..."

"Are you hypnotizing me again?"

"It's not quite hypnosis... But if you like, we can call it that. Close your eyes and relax... Okay, we're starting."

Iren drew back curtains as white as her blouse and thoughtfully watched me leave the building. She took her phone in hand. "Hello."

"Yes, it's me. So, what's up?"

"No real progress..."

"Yeah, you should just slip him a woman."

"He's not interested in women..."

"Is he gay?"

"I tried to convince him he's a latent homosexual... Didn't work."

"So what does he really want?"

"His project. And... a bit of revenge on those who ruined his life."

"What?," the voice on the phone roared. "He's crazy... Doesn't he blame himself for all his failures?"

"He does... for trusting people he shouldn't have. To some extent, he's obsessed... I told him it's time to let it all go and live for today... Tried to appeal to his reason... He says a war only ends when one side surrenders. He's not ready to give up yet."

"Does he know about us?"

"He suspects..."

"Then we'll have to finish him off... If this leaks out... Prison awaits us, and for a very long time... With asset confiscation. We'll have to give up our fancy cars... And many of us won't live to see the trial. Do you understand that?"

"I do... I don't have a car, let alone a fancy one like you."

"You have a luxury apartment and an office downtown... And your rich and influential clients... And your eldest son in America..."

"...a low-profile job, it seems, at a Jewish Agency, which can be easily lost, just like the Green Card. And the younger one..."

"Enough! What are you suggesting?"

"Better to get rid of this obsessive neat freak in Akmol rather than in the capital... Less noise and dust there... It's a shame we didn't do it sooner... Tell him to move to another city."

"Wait, I have an idea..."

The voice on the phone rasped. Someone coughed and then blew their nose loudly. Then came the words: "Fine. Just don't drag this out... I'm running out of rope here... It's time to end this show."

The call disconnected.

Iren stepped away from the window and sat down in her office chair. Staring at a single point in the room, she lit a cigarette and slowly blew out rings of smoke.

How slowly step the horses,
How faint the lanterns' light!
Strangers surely know
Where they carry me tonight.

I yield myself to their care.
I'm cold, and longing for sleep;
We jolted on a corner sharp,
Into a starbeam deep.

A fevered head's soft nodding,
A stranger's hand so cold,
The dark firs' unfamiliar forms—
A sight yet to unfold.

—Osip Mandelstam

X. The Flash Drive

The phone rang.

"Hello?"

"Good afternoon! This is the trauma department at Soroka Hospital calling."

"How can I help you?"

"Are you acquainted with Dmitry Zazhinsky?"

"Dmitry?" I hesitated, not immediately realizing they meant Dima. "Oh, Dmitry," it finally clicked. "Yes, of course!"

"He asked you to come see him."

"What happened?"

"He was attacked by hooligans and beaten. He was admitted to us last night with multiple broken ribs and limbs, as well as head injuries. Luckily, some passersby noticed and called an ambulance…"

"I'll definitely come to see him."

***

A light spring rain was drizzling, the kind of rare seasonal rain that Concordia's nature gifted before the dry, hot summer set in… I climbed the steps to the main building of Soroka Hospital. Exiting the elevator on the fifth floor, I entered the ward where Dima was.

123

"Hello, Dima." Dima, wrapped in plaster casts with his leg and arms suspended, managed only a faint smile.

"Dima, what's the matter, my friend?"

"A drawer," Dima answered weakly.

"What does a drawer have to do with anything, Dima?"

"My jacket, the right pocket..."

"Alright," I said, opening the drawer and carefully taking out a neatly folded jacket.

"A flash drive." I slipped my hand into the right pocket of the jacket and felt the flash drive.

"Why would I need this?" I asked, surprised.

"There's a file with a list of Kainman's fabricated articles," Dima said slowly, swallowing hard. "We'll send it to the American Academy of Sciences."

"You really think the academics will do anything about it?"

"I hope so. There's also a list of grants that...," he paused, "Kainman got based on those articles. Each NIH RO1 grant, as you know, is about three million dollars."

"Alright, I'll send it."

"Thank you. I always believed in you."

A nurse quietly entered the room and asked me to step outside. "He's very weak. He mustn't get upset," she said. I left the ward. It was hard to process everything in my mind. The flash drive. Dima. Last night's dinner at the bar. Kainman... I turned the flash drive over in my hand and slipped it into my jeans pocket. The rain had stopped, and a friendly spring sun peeked out from behind the clouds.

On the street, motorcyclists raced by on their battle "horses" ... In black jackets and decorated helmets, they could easily be mistaken for heavy knight cavalry...

Shoppers crowded around the supermarket. They looked like watchful infantrymen patrolling castle walls. And at the castle gates, that is, the supermarket entrance, they busily rustled swords and spears, or rather, bags of groceries...

I hate the light
Of monotonous stars.
Hello, my long-time madness—
The pointed growth of towers!

Become lace, stone,
And turn to cobwebs,
Pierce the empty breast of the sky
With a thin needle's wound!

My turn will come—
I feel the wings unfold.
But where will the arrow of living thought
Fly off to?

Or having spent my path and time,
Will I return?
There—I could not love,
Here—I am afraid to love...

—Osip Mandelstam

XI. The Voice of Freedom

Vasily Grossman wrote in his book *Life and Fate* that true, far-reaching discoveries happen when a scientist breathes freely. For a long time, I couldn't explain the results of my experiments... It seemed the protein complex assembled on the mitochondrial membrane. But not all the mediators involved in that specific signaling pathway were present in the complex. And crucially, the main enzyme, which was the whole fuss, was missing. I couldn't understand why. Kainman was nervous too: "Volodya, we'll be nailed to the wall if we don't find an explanation..." But the explanation didn't come.

Exhausted both by the impossibility of finishing the project and the endless lab dramas, I took a short vacation and went to Concordia, to my mother...

Holding back tears, my mother listened as I told her about America. I spoke of snowy peaks over Lake Tahoe, ice skating on the frozen mountain lake during a scientific conference at the Keystone ski resort, the water park in sunny Orlando, the geysers shooting from underground and massive Grizzly bears in Yellowstone National Park, and the Pacific sea lions...

"And how's work?" my mother asked cautiously.

"Everything's fine," I tried to sound upbeat. "The project is moving forward... The boss is very smart. His students work hard and are committed to collaboration..."

"Will you stay in the States?"

"I can't say yet... But I already have a Green Card... We'll see if I can find a job in America."

"Can your boss help you with anything?"

"I don't know. I don't want to bother him... The paper isn't published yet..."

"Well, God willing, everything will work out..."

In recent years, my mother had become somewhat devout... She lit candles on Saturdays and said prayers... Once a year, she would travel to Akmol to visit her mother-in-law's grave, asking a rabbi to say a prayer.

In the evenings, when nature and the earth in Concordia rested from the heat, I walked around town with my mother. At her request, I told her again and again about America, the lost mountain national parks, and the glittering skyscrapers of big cities...

During one of those walks, it struck me: "It's a multistep system... There are at least three complexes on the mitochondria... And although I don't yet know where the second and third complexes are located, it's as obvious as having ice cream after lunch..."

Only while on vacation did I understand how the enzyme on the mitochondrial membrane is activated.

But I didn't yet know that my manuscript would be published nowhere... Kainman "didn't get the green light" ...

Where Roman judges judged a foreign people,
Stands a basilica, joyous and proud
Like Adam once, its nerves outspread,
The vaulted crosslight arches play aloud.

Yet from without, a secret plan betrays,
Here, the strength of flying buttresses cares,
So the massive weight of walls won't crush,
And the bold vault stands free from battering bears.

A labyrinth wild, a forest profound,
A reasoned abyss of Gothic souls,
Egyptian might with Christian's timid ground,
Beside a reed, an oak, and kingly roles.

But the more I studied Notre Dame's frame,
Your monstrous ribs, the fortress' spine,
The more I thought: from heavy, cruel weight,
One day I too would create something fine...

—Osip Mandelstam

XII. Mother

Grumbling is not the biggest flaw, but it is quite noticeable. You, dear reader, have probably grown weary of my endless list of complaints... But were there any other days in my short scientific life? Didn't I experience catharsis when something finally worked in my experiments? Of course! Successful experiments that lifted my spirits and gave me hope often distracted me from the laboratory "curiosities," like the tips of Jacqueline's fancy shoes she wore on her frequent dates; the foggy, dirty double glasses of William Roshti as he "puffed" over yet another grant, already knowing he wouldn't get it for scientific reasons; the dark dentures (or their absence) of Rachel Baldakhinov-Shavit, which she bared when she flew into a furious rage; and who or what else?...

"Don't shut yourself in," my mother said, "give me your hand." My poor mother. She fainted while giving blood to earn extra vacation days and come see me in...

Saratov. She shared her last piece of bread with me during my early years in Concordia and when I served in the Concordian army. She worked day and night as a nurse in a hospital, with a single goal: to earn enough for us to have even a tiny apartment. And when I mentioned over the phone that I was having problems in America, she immediately rushed from Concordia to San Francisco and supported me behind the scenes...

I had long realized that my phone and home conversations were being monitored and passed on to Kainman, Olezhek, and Jacqueline. So we made it clear to each other that we needed to talk outside.

Once we were at a safe distance from my apartment, I said: "I'm going back to Concordia."

"Are you sure you want to go back? Maybe you can negotiate with Kainman? After all, he's also from Concordia..."

"No. That's impossible. I gave him everything except the main project... But he is obsessed with crushing me. Kainman told me I must give up the project... Nobody in America wants to hire me... And it's all because of him. I've been hinted at this more than once..."

And hesitating a little, I continued: "Can I stay with you for a while?"

"That too," she sorrowfully threw up her hands.

"I'll just find a job and move to another apartment."

"Relax. Let's go pack your things instead." She said, hugging me by the shoulders.

And now, when I feel bad, I close my eyes and see you, my dear mother, as a child. Summer. I squirm in my chair, choking on hateful semolina porridge in a little house by the river. There your chintz yellow-black dress flashes, fluttering among the trees. And I clearly see your small, thin, fragile figure. I jump up and run to meet you, almost knocking over grandmother, who was cooking in the kitchen... Where are you rushing to, you little rascal? But I just shout back to grandmother: She's come!

Who? Who arrived? My mother. Tears streaming down my face, I ran into her arms. "Why were you gone so long, Mama?"

"I was at work," she answered with a smile.

In life, anything can happen. A lover may stop loving you... A job that once seemed unshakable, a respected place in society, the regard of colleagues, can all vanish overnight, without warning and without return. But a mother's love is stronger than all of it. It doesn't depend on success or failure. It is eternal.

Alas, dear reader, there will be no poetry this time. But if you'd like... turn on the orchestra of Paul Mauriat. The piece is simply called: "Mama."

XIII. Job Interview

Right after speaking with my mother, I called Professor Alberto Manay, a specialist in rheumatology. I had previously received a scholarship for work in that field, and I hoped it might help me secure a position in his lab.

"Hello, is this Professor Manay's office? I'm calling about the lab assistant position listed on your institute's website."

"Yes. Please come in tomorrow. And be sure to watch both ways when crossing the street."

"Thank you very much."

"No, thank you," the secretary added with unexpected insistence.

I hung up the phone.

The next day, I made my way to Professor Manay's office. But even as I climbed the long steps toward the isolated building, tucked inside a ring of parking lots, I felt an inexplicable sense of unease. It was as if something ominous was hanging in the air.

The multi-story building, topped with a sharp spire pointing skyward, was painted a dull, oppressive gray. Its pseudo-Gothic architecture, built in the 1930s, resembled more a fortress from a dark fantasy than a research institute. Narrow, elongated windows with faint, lifeless light only reinforced its grim façade.

And then it struck me: the building was an exact replica of the medical faculty building I had once worked in, back in Denver.

Inside, however, the mood flipped. The lobby was blindingly bright, almost aggressively sterile. Students and junior researchers bustled back and forth, the energy palpable. I merged into the crowd and shuffled along the polished floor toward the elevators.

Standing beside the elevator was an elderly woman, athletic-looking for her age, dressed in a tailored suit made of...

Dressed in a blue blazer and matching trousers, she looked at me through her large glasses and said in a deep, throaty voice, with great importance:

"Look at the book."

"What's its name?"

"Moscow's rules"

"No, thanks."

"...That's a pity," gurgled the woman in blue.

I shrugged and stepped into the elevator. The heavy double metal doors groaned shut behind me, and the lift began to ascend to the third floor.

"To visit the three beauties..." hissed a mysterious voice.

When I stepped out, slightly dazed, the corridor seemed to shimmer. I could swear Saruman himself was winking at me, his jade prayer beads slipping through his fingers. His starry cloak whispered and howled as it drifted along the hallway behind him.

I shook my head, waved my arms, spat three times over my left shoulder, and stomped my foot, chasing away the vision. Saruman, the beads, and the robe disappeared. Reality snapped back into place, solid, grounded, and ordinary once more.

With a steady stride, I entered the office of Professor Alberto Manay.

"Why didn't you mention you worked with Sergio Kainman?"

Manay's eyes lit up with excitement. "I have great admiration for his talent; he's a friend of mine. One of his students worked here briefly. A bit of a collaboration, you could say. I believe his name was Hans... I taught him a thing or two," he added with a wink.

"It was as if Alberto was already trying to justify himself, apparently expecting to be accused of plagiarism."

Only now did I understand why Hans had smiled at me that way when he left Kainman's office... and why my fellowship wasn't renewed for another year, despite the fact that I had completed the overwhelming majority of the work outlined in the scientific proposal."

"And what are you working on?"

"I'm studying the role of mitochondria in Death Receptor Signaling... I wrote to you about this."

"Are you schizophrenic?"

"Excuse me?"

"Are you mentally ill?"

I paused, regretting I hadn't brought a recording device. "Fine. We'll see during your lecture what you've done..."

It was a rather strange demand, to give a seminar as part of an interview for a lab assistant position...

I spoke into a terrifying silence. After the talk, no one asked a single question. Everyone simply stood up and silently walked out of the room.

The emboldened Manai deftly snatched his laptop from my hands, the one I had copied my presentation file onto. So, I didn't even

I didn't even manage to delete the file. (Before the presentation, I was asked to transfer the file from my flash drive to their laptop, because, allegedly, the drive's adapter had to be urgently returned to the department office.)

Although, to be honest, what Hans had already told him was probably more than enough...

I didn't get the job. But two years later, Manai published a paper on the very same transporter, the one I had discussed during my seminar in his lab. Before and after that publication, there hadn't been a single paper by Alberto Manai on mitochondrial transporters...

Rain, or maybe hail, pounded loudly against the windows. The wind bent defenseless trees, their leaves fluttering helplessly as if surprised by this unseasonal storm. The sky was wrapped in thick gray clouds that seemed to blanket the whole planet. Both above and below, a tempest reigned. The gods hurled lightning bolts and deafening thunder alongside the torrents of rain and biting wind.

I wrapped myself in a warm, itchy woolen blanket and sank into an old creaky armchair in front of the TV. I couldn't find the words to fully express the inner storm that had, little by little, begun to settle, just as the glass of cognac in my hand emptied. I felt warm again, closed my eyes, and fell asleep.

I dreamt of a summer on the Desna River, in Ukraine. (Yes, '*On*' Ukraine, not '*In*' because that's how my grandmother used to say it, and no matter how much history is rewritten, I reserve the right to the grammar of the language I grew up with.)

not *in*. I don't accept that.

So, there I am, running along the canal with a noisy bunch of friends. One of us calls out, and without any agreement, we all quickly strip off our clothes and jump into the water.

"Whoever swims to the opposite shore first gets to ride my brand-new bike all day tomorrow!" I hear someone say.

And now I'm swimming with all my might, flailing my arms wide, gasping for air, splashing water everywhere. The bright rays of the midday sun beat down on my face, blinding me a little. Ahead, the other shore is waiting for me.

There, the other shore awaits.

The merry flag flies high on the mast—
Like a beacon's flame aglow.
The sail is sinking,
The sail is sinking,
Beyond the horizon's flow.

Colors dance upon the waves,
And light leaps like a dolphin's play...
It's like a fairy tale,
It's like a fairy tale,
No other such display.

But suddenly the sea grows fierce—
That's the temper oceans show.
Where are you going, sail?
Where are you going, sail?
Come back soon, come back soon, I know!

Yet the sail flared bright and slipped away,
Not a word was heard from it.
And I don't know,
And I don't know,
If it was there or just a myth.

—Rimma Kazakova

XIV. Eternal Rest

Étienne gently and tenderly stroked his horse's mane. The horse occasionally nodded approvingly. From the sparsely forested hilltop, a majestic view unfolded: an ancient castle, a green valley, and the sea.

For two years, Étienne and his loyal squire François wandered across Europe, covering their tracks and evading their pursuers... Two years of hardship, skirmishes, and narrow escapes. Finally, they arrived in Scotland.

"Well, François, here we are. This is where we'll hide the Grail from all the rulers of the world."

"Why here?" François asked, puzzled.

"Where else? Not in the French king's palace, surely?" Étienne smiled. "We thoroughly lost our pursuers after exposing ourselves in Milan and Prague..."

"But still, why here, in this abandoned castle?"

"You ask questions with no answer or with very simple explanations... Why, for example, do the Jews count days from Passover to Shavuot and from Shavuot to Rosh Hashanah in multiples of seven? Or why is their festival of Hanukkah in December, not June?"

"Well, that's easy. There are seven days in a week. And December days are short, so more light is needed.

Hence a festival of candles. And by the way, Christmas is also in December..."

"Exactly, François. The forces of nature merged with the forces of history. That's the foundation of the Tanakh... Scotland is far from France. The sea divides them... And in this ancient castle, no one would think to look for the Grail."

"But maybe the Holy Grail could benefit someone?"

"To whom? To cruel, treacherous rulers? Or to elites mired in ignorance and debauchery? No, François, humanity is not yet ready to possess it."

"But then I have a question: does the Holy Grail truly have miraculous powers?"

"Whether it does or not is unknown. To me, it is a symbol of the Templars' steadfastness, of freedom and free will. The Grail must never fall into the hands of the executioner..."

"The miraculous nature of the Grail is a matter of faith. After all, I don't ask you: whom do you trust more, the Pharisees or the Sadducees?"

"The Pharisees were merchants in the temple. Their level of education is questionable, and the Sadducees insisted there is no afterlife or resurrection. Therefore, no miracle of the Messiah. That is heresy and blasphemy!"

"Who knows, François. Who knows. In one thing you're right, a little education never hurts… This is what the ancient Greek philosophers believed."

At that moment, François spat out some berries, cursing:

"God, that's disgusting!"

"Told you, don't eat just anything!"

"I haven't eaten since yesterday morning. My stomach's already growling," François muttered indignantly, wiping his mouth with his sleeve.

"Now," Étienne continued without listening, "Democritus said: 'Nothing exists except atoms and empty space; everything else is opinion.' The great Socrates declared: 'I know one thing: that I know nothing. This is the source of my wisdom.' And the incomparable Thales left us this commandment: 'A happy man is one with a healthy body, a rich soul, and a well-educated mind.' Finally, Epictetus noted that only educated people are truly free."

"Good heavens, but you're quoting pagans!" François interjected.

"Yes, and they were some of the wisest men. Quiet! Do you see those people by the castle gate? Let's hide behind those pines…"

Below, a dozen armed riders were bustling about. One approached the gate and, without dismounting, fiercely knocked on the door.

"In the name of the King of France, open up!"

A disheveled head poked out from the tower's arrow slit.

"You're in Scotland. The laws of the King of France do not apply here..."

"I have a charter signed by Robert I, King of Scotland. You are obliged to assist us..." With these words, he unfolded the document and extended his hand toward the tower.

"We owe you nothing. Get lost..." The disheveled head disappeared.

"My lord, there's no one here...," one of the knights broke in. "Who would think to come to this wilderness? Let's ride to Edinburgh. We'll have lunch there."

The one who had knocked angrily struck the castle wall with his whip, turned his horse, and commanded his retinue:

"To Edinburgh!"

Étienne and François waited a moment before emerging from their hiding place.

"No more doubts! They're waiting for us there! Forward, François!"

Étienne adjusted the Grail tucked beneath his coat, urged his horse onward, waved to François, and the two slowly descended the mountain slope on their obedient steeds

www.ingramcontent.com/pod-product-compliance
Lightning Source LLC
Chambersburg PA
CBHW040829010826
48978CB00012BB/668